Ceremony

Ceremony

First published in Indonesian under the title *Upacara: Sebuah Novel* by Pustaka Jaya.
Korrie Layun Rampan, (Jakarta: Grasindo—PT Gramedia Widiasarana Indonesa, 2007)
English translation copyright © 2014 George A. Fowler
English language edition copyright © 2014 The Lontar Foundation

Publication of the Modern Library of Indonesia Series, of which this book is one title,
has been made possible by the generous assistance of The Djarum Foundation.
The cost of translation for this book was covered by a grant from
the Ministry of Education and Culture of the Republic of Indonesia.

Template design by DesignLab; layout and cover by Cyprianus Jaya Napiun
Cover illustration: detail from *The Process 10,* by Mella Jaarsma.
Image courtesy of John H McGlynn.

Printed in Indonesia by PT Suburmitra Grafistama

ISBN No. 978-979-8083-96-9

KORRIE LAYUN RAMPAN

Ceremony

translated by
George A Fowler

with an introduction by
Bernard Sellato

Jakarta, Indonesia

Contents

Introduction, *vii*

Translator's Note and Acknowledgments, *xvi*

Glossary, *xx*

Ceremony

I.   Climbing Mount Lumut: Ascending To Heaven, *2*

II. Balian, *26*

III. Kewangkey: Burying the Bones, *64*

IV. Nalin Taun: The Ceremony of Offering, *82*

V.   Pelulung: The Marriage Ceremony, *108*

A Brief Note by the Author After the Passage of
    Thirty Years, *119*

Foreword to the Original Indonesian Edition by Dodong
    Djiwapradja, *123*

Additional Reading Material, *133*

Biographical Information, *137*

Introduction

Borneo

The island of Borneo is a huge land mass, covering some 750,000 square kilometers—three times the surface of the United Kingdom and significantly larger than Texas. Two thirds of its territory forms the Indonesian provinces of Kalimantan, the northern third being divided between the Malaysian states of Sabah and Sarawak and the tiny sultanate of Brunei Darussalam. The island's population remains relatively low, with an estimated twenty million people unevenly distributed across it.

Coastal regions feature towns connected to the maritime trade, while the interior is home to small tribal groups relying on self-subsistence, hill-rice agriculture. This contrast has historically set apart the lowland Malays and the hinterland Dayak. Lowland regions witnessed the emergence of early trading ports, originally under tribal chieftains' control, later to become Indianized kingdoms, probably in the first centuries of the Christian era, then Islamized sultanates after the mid-second millennium. In the course of time, some Dayak groups in the middle reaches of rivers also converted to Islam, a process that is still ongoing, whereas many upper-river groups were later Christianized during the colonial period, and some retained their traditional religions.

While lowland Malay cultures are relatively homogeneous around the island, there are several major ethnic groupings among the Dayak, differing in languages, but showing common features in their cosmology, social organization, funerary practices and fertility cults, and material culture.

The Benuaq

The Benuaq people, one of the largest ethnic groups of Kutai Barat regency in East Kalimantan, occupy the southern tributaries of the middle course of the Mahakam River along the border with Central Kalimantan province—the Bongan, Ohong, Jelau, Kelawit, Tuang, Lawa, Kedang Pahu, and Nyuatan rivers—as well as around the Jempang Lake area and the town of Tenggarong, with some in the upper Teweh River drainage in Central Kalimantan. As of 2012, the Benuaq of the various river-based sub-groups, each with a distinctive dialect, may altogether number as many as 40,000.

Linguistically as well as culturally, the Benuaq, together with the Luangan (or Lawangan) of Central Kalimantan and the Paser (or Pasir) of southern East Kalimantan, constitute a larger grouping, which itself belongs to the important Barito Dayak cluster, including the Ngaju, Ma'anyan, and Ot Danum.

The Benuaq believe that they have always lived in the region they occupy today, although their ultimate origin, as mentioned in their myths, may be the Mt Lumut area, to the south, which retains a crucial role in their cosmology. The name Benuaq comes from *benua*, a term meaning "land" or "territory". While it is likely that one particular local ethnic sub-group of the lower Mahakam stood at the origin of the kingdom of Kutai and became Orang Kutai (Kutai people), the rest of them became the Orang Benua, "the people of the land", and formed its productive basis (rice farming and the collection of forest products). As the kingdom's historical limit extended only to Muara Pahu, these Orang Benua, the king's people, contrasted with independent ("wild") Dayak groups farther upriver.

Benuaq people today identify as Dayak, in contrast to neighboring Muslim peoples; or as Benuaq, in contrast to other Dayak groups; or, among themselves, by reference to the river drainage where they live, for example, Benuaq Ohookng (Ohong). In the context of the recent administrative and economic decentralization policies, allowing for strong political and cultural revitalization, local differences tend to fade away, and ethnic politics and identity are gaining momentum.

Economy and Society

The Benuaq, often viewed as subsistence dry-rice farmers, actually practice a complex combination of economic pursuits, since the soils of their region are relatively poor. Historically, their strategies grew out of the trade in forest products, the most important of which now are rattan and rubber, sometimes collected in the forest, but mainly grown in gardens. They also grow other products, such as fruits, in forest gardens (*simpung* or *lembo*). Today, off-farm work like logging, fishing, gold washing, and various types of wage labor are also part of their economic system.

Most Benuaq settlements traditionally consisted of a longhouse (*lou*), which included any number of family apartments (*olang* or *pokan*; Korrie's *bilik*), each with its hearth and inhabited by an extended, three-generational family headed by a *tuha pokan*. Today, most villages comprise individual family houses, although some still have a longhouse, which is often used for meetings and large rituals, or as a tourist attraction.

The old Benuaq society distinguished several social categories: the nobility or royalty, *manti* (or *mantiiq*); ordinary, free-born people, *merendika* (or *marantika*); and persons in bondage: debt-slaves, *ripan*, and war captives, *batang ulun*. An intermediate category, *pengawa* (or *pengkawar*), served as a buffer between nobles and free men and filled certain supervisory positions. These names derived from the kingdom's vocabulary, for example, *manti* from *menteri*, *merendika* from *merdeka*. Today, of course, the slave categories have disappeared, and hardly any difference in living standards stresses otherwise invisible distinctions of status between free men and nobles, although the position of religious leader (*kepala adat*) is usually held by a member of a royal or noble lineage (*katurunan*).

Kinship is cognatic and its terminology is bilateral, that is, descent is traced through both father's and mother's lines. Young couples usually reside with the bride's parents, then set up house on their own, and women enjoy a high social status. All children have the same inheritance rights in the case of land (rice fields or forest gardens). Many aspects of social life, as well as of land tenure, are regulated by *adat*, the unwritten law handed down from one generation to the next and supervised by the *kepala adat* and acknowledged elders. Cases of breach of *adat* are discussed in meetings (*besara*) until a consensus is found, leading to fines and ritual payments.

Cosmology and Religion

Benuaq cosmology is described in myths (*tempun*) recited during major ceremonies, such as *nguguq taun* and *kwangkay*, by ritual specialists, the *pembelian* and *pengewara*. Although it seems that, in the past, a small group of primordial deities were known (Kayangan, Perjadiiq, Lantalah), one of them has emerged, maybe due to contact with monotheistic neighbors, as a high god, creator and ruler of the world, and variously called Lantalah, Lahtala, or Letalla (Korrie's Letala)—although yet other gods are mentioned, such as Jewata, the water god, or Tonoy, the earth god. Under the high god, the *sengiang* (or *seniang*; Korrie's *senieng*), minor deities, spirits, or elementary forces, inhabit the various layers of heaven, and are invoked in major rituals. The *nyahuq, mulung, tangkai,* or *ntuh*, benevolent spirits viewed as supportive of human enterprise, intervene, through the *pembelian* priests, as mediators between humans and the *sengiang* to request good fortune or to bar evil spirits' influence. Those malevolent spirits, *mulang*, *blis*, or *papaiq*, believed to dwell in nature (plants, water) or in people (witches), may cause sickness, epidemics, and misfortune and must be removed.

In humans, the Benuaq distinguish between a vital force (*jus* or *semangat*) and an intellectual faculty, the latter located in the head. At death, both leave the body as *roh*, a generic term. The intellect becomes a *kelelungan*, a shapeless spell, and proceeds to Tenangkai, a place on a mountain top, to await the time of the final funerary ritual. The *semangat* becomes a *liau*, a spirit of similar physiological constitution as humans, which requires food, drink, and entertainment and can feel pain and emotions, and remains to roam in the neighborhood of the grave or the deceased person's home. The *liau* eventually reaches Gunung Lumut (Mt Lumut) to be weighed for its deeds before being allowed to continue to Lewu Liau, its final abode.

Until World War II, the religion of the "Barito Dayak"— Ngaju, Luangan, Ma'anyan, Benuaq, Ot Danum—had no specific name, being referred to just as "the old religion". Missionaries of the colonial period viewed these people as "heathens". The name Kaharingan to refer to the old religion seems to have emerged during the Japanese occupation. It derived from *haring*, meaning "self-existent" or "source", the word *kaharingan* then referring to a "source of life" or "life force". The Indonesian government did not recognize Kaharingan as a religion, and many of its followers had to declare themselves Christians or Muslims. In the 1970s, traditional leaders lobbied to have Kaharingan recognized by the State, which they finally obtained in March 1980. Kaharingan is now classified, along with Balinese Hinduism, in the Hindu Dharma category (although, to this day, the Benuaq still seldom use the word Kaharingan). In any event, some of the Benuaq are now Christians, while in some areas (Kota Bangun, Bongan,

Jembayan, Ohong), Benuaq communities, under pressure from neighboring Muslim (Kutai) communities and the administration, have converted to Islam, thus becoming Orang Kutai.

Rituals of Life and Death

Benuaq religious life is basically organized in a dual pattern: rituals for the living (various kinds of shamanic *belian* ceremonies) and rituals for the dead (several stages, up to the final *kwangkay*). But agricultural rituals also exist. The religious practices of the Benuaq are an integral part of their adat. Although it now has a "holy book" and somewhat standardized religious practices, this "old religion", as an orally transmitted belief system, traditionally comprised neither formal written texts nor the worship of deities. Instead, great importance lies on spirits, which can have impact on peoples' lives. In spite of Christianization, Islamization, and modernization, traditional rituals still play a vital role in Benuaq villages in Kutai Barat. These rituals reveal some variation in the detail of their unfolding among the Benuaq sub-groups, as well as dialectal variation in their names.

Rituals for the Living

The word *belian* (or *balian*) refers to rituals meant to remove evil from persons or communities and restore the balance between humans and the cosmos when it has been disturbed. There are three major categories of *belian* ceremonies: *belian lowangan* (or *luangan*; Korrie's *balian lawangan*) are village-wide purification rites, formerly held yearly; *belian beneq* focus on divination and curing; and *belian bawe* (women's *beliatn*) are concerned with the health and welfare of mothers and children and with their purification. These categories, however, are somewhat porous and similar rituals may be held in different circumstances in different regions.

The *belian lowangan* category includes several types, among which the *nguguq taun* (or *guguq*; Korrie's *erau ngugu taun*), the highest *belian* ceremony, has a threefold purpose: to thank the *sengiang* for a successful year, a good harvest, or good health in the village; to invoke the benevolent spirits to prevent epidemics, crop failure, pests, and famine in the coming year; and to purify the village and its fields from evil caused by some violation of taboo (*tuhing*). It often covers several aspects, such as curing (*nalin rotan*) and purifying (*melas taun*; Korrie's *nalin taun*). It usually lasts sixteen nights and requires the sacrifice of a water buffalo.

The *belian beneq* comprises three closely related types of small curing rituals: *belian senteo* (or *sentiu*; Korrie's *senteau*) is the only variant practiced on the Bongan, Ohong, Kelawit, and lower Pahu; *belian bawo*, said to originate in Central Kalimantan, is found in the Nyuatan area; and the *belian beneq* proper, the "common *belian*" (also called *belian turaan* or *belian timeeq*). Higher (and longer) rituals, such as *bekeleeu*, may involve a combination of two or more of these, and a *belian bawe*, and may be held after the sick person has recovered.

Belian bawe rituals are performed by female *pembelian*. Most are held during pregnancy, childbirth, and nursing. They include the *nyamat butung*, during pregnancy; the *ngejakat* or *belian jiwata* (or *jewata*), immediately after childbirth; the *tempong pusong* or *belian turaan*, one week after birth, when the umbilical cord falls; the *ngenus* bathing ritual on the fortieth day; the *turun tana* ritual, when the child is made to touch the ground for the first time; and the *belian melas kanak* (Korrie's *meles*), when the child reaches the age of five. Wedding rites, *beripun* (see Korrie's *pelulung*) are also part of the female ritual sphere, and female *pembelian* may also perform various types of "common *belian*" ceremonies.

Rituals for the Dead

Rituals for the dead are held in three stages: the *parem api* is the transfer of the body to a wooden coffin (*lungun*), held right after death, and lasts up to one week; the *kenyauw* (or *kenyeu*), held after a few years, involves the removal of the body, the separation of flesh and bones (*nulang*), and the storing of the bones in a temporary burial structure (*rinaq*); and the *kwangkay* (or *kewangkey*), held whenever the family has been able to gather the necessary funds, is the final stage, and a prominent event in Benuaq religious and social life.

The *kwangkay* itself is divided into several stages, culminating in the journey of the *liau* to heaven. In a first phase, a religious specialist, the *wara* (or *pengewara*), calls the *liau* of ancestors, which may take days or weeks; then, recurrent offerings of food are made to these spirits, accompanied with dances (*ngerangkau*); a final phase consists of animal sacrifices (chickens, pigs, and at least one water buffalo), food offerings to and entertainment for the spirits, the dispatching of the deceased's *liau*, guided and accompanied on its way by the *wara*, to its resting place, Lewu Liau, and the deposition of the bones in a special funerary monument (*teplaq*; Korrie's *tempelaq*).

The Benuaq believe that the status of the *liau* in Lewu Liau depends on the completion of the *kwangkay* by the living— immediate family and the broad network of relatives. Considerable amounts of money are needed to be able to hold such a ceremony, which may last from one week up to two months: sacrificial animals have to be raised or bought in numbers (in the past, a human sacrifice was necessary, later replaced by a buffalo); large amounts of rice and other consumables must be prepared to feed spirits, guests, family, and performers for such a prolonged period; a *wara* must be hired to perform all necessary rituals, and gifts bought for him; additional gifts have to be made to the ancestral spirits. Specialists must be hired to carve the funerary monuments: the *belontanq*, a carved post to which the sacrificial buffalo is tied; the *selimat*, a container for the skulls of the ancestors during the ceremony; and the *tepla*, a carved sarcophagus where the bones of the dead are laid to rest at the end of the ceremony.

Such costly ceremonies are held mainly for members of the upper social categories, whose *liau* must be given VIP treatment; and yet it may be many years before the families can afford to hold a *kwangkay*. This extravagant display of mourning also contributes to raising the social prestige of a family—which may be deeply in debt by the time the ceremony is over. Death in Benuaq society is a dynamic force stimulating the economic activities of the living, periodically reactivating and tightening kin and social networks, and maintaining open the relational channels between the living and their ancestors.

Farming Rituals

A number of rituals related to the cycle of the paddy used to be performed: to find a suitable plot of land to clear a field (*eraang*); to plant the rice seed (*ngasek*); to please the rice spirit (*lolang luing*); to bring in the first young rice; to feed the *nyahuq* spirits (*pakan nyahuq*); to recall the rice spirit (*ngeluing*); to prevent a drought (*nular*) or pest infestation; and finally to purify the land and forest after the harvest (*nguguq taun*). Many of them, however, are now rapidly falling into disuse.

As is clear from the pages above—and from Korrie Layun Rampan's novel—Benuaq life is a highly ritualized one, in all spheres of human activity, in the life cycle as in the farming cycle.

Bernard Sellato

Translator's Note and Acknowledgments

The translator faces two distinct and challenging aspects of *Upacara* (*Ceremony*) by Korrie Layun Rampan, Indonesian Dayak poet-novelist, literary renaissance man and in recent years, political watchdog, and finally, politician. First, the rather massive number of Benuaq Dayak language terms that appear in this relatively short novel (113 pages in my source, the 2007 Grasindo edition). Second, the author's complex style, which effortlessly ranges from the edgy and clipped (as befits the youthful narrator-protagonist) to the discursive, erotically ecstatic and lyrical, to the nightmarishly visionary.

The Grasindo edition includes a helpful 104-word glossary of culturally technical terms related to the daily life and religious outlook and practices of the Benuaq people of East Kalimantan. For a translator, that is a good start, but there are still plenty of such terms in the text that for some reason didn't make it into the glossary. Internet searches produced explanations or hints of explanations, mostly in Indonesian, for a few of these. Luckily, I was ultimately able to refer all terminology-related questions to several native speakers of Benuaq, including, notably, the author himself (see Acknowledgements). As it turned out, several of these terms were explained to me in more than one way.

In order to harness this plethora of Benuaq words to vividly evoke the cultural ambiance of the novel (as, I believe, was the author's intention), but without overwhelming the reader and jeopardizing a smooth read, I have expanded the text slightly, and I hope, unobtrusively, to incorporate explanations of most of these terms when they occur. In fact, the author did this himself in several places. When such terms recurred at some degree of separation throughout the text, I have provided entries for them in a new glossary I have put together, which for the most part is a combination of the Grasindo glossary and the explanations provided by native speakers. Finally, some terms that I considered of lesser importance, I simply glossed in English without presenting them in Benuaq.

As to Korrie Layun Rampan's writing style, suffice it to say that one of my professional translator colleagues, a native speaker of Indonesian, with whom I discussed certain problematic aspects of this translation, said in effect, "Pak Korrie's writing, sometimes mysterious, but always interesting." Correct on both scores. I would only add, more than just interesting, but writing with surprising impact. I have tried to convey not only the correct reading of this story, of course, but also the rhythms, tone, and "punch" of his unusual style.

There is much love interest in this story. Like American sweethearts with their "Daddy" and "Baby" (at least in song), Indonesian lovers often address each other as "Kakak" or "Kak" or "Abang", meaning "Older Sibling" or "Brother", and "Adik" or "Dik", meaning "Younger Sibling" or "Sister", rather than saying each other's name, and this practice is very much in evidence in *Ceremony*.

I have also included from the Grasindo edition Korrie Layun Rampan's own thirty-year retrospective note on writing *Upacara* and then winning the 1976 Jakarta Arts Council's Novel Writing Contest, together with a critical analysis of this novel by Dodong Djiwapradja, one of the five members of the Jury Council of this contest. Readers who find themselves somewhat mystified by the non-linear narrative will undoubtedly find Bapak Dodong's analysis helpful.

Finally, since it is likely that neither the Dayak people, nor the island of Borneo will be very familiar to Western readers of *Ceremony*, renowned expert on the cultures, languages, arts, and history of Kalimantan, Dr Bernard Sellato has generously provided an introduction that will, I hope, provide in broad strokes the geographical, historical, and cultural setting of this novel.

*

Numerous people helped me in my translation of *Upacara*. First and foremost, I would like to thank the author, Bapak Korrie Layun Rampan, for his patient and illuminating response to my questions concerning references and Benuaq language terms in the novel. Similarly, through Lontar, I was able to contact Dr Sellato, who in turn forwarded a list of my queries to two Benuaq Dayak friends, Bapak Paulus Kadok and Bapak Tengkon, *adat* authorities at Kampung Lamikng, Muara Lawa, West Kutai Regency, East Kalimantan. The responses I received from Paulus and Tengkon were also gratifyingly detailed and to-the-point.

As on previous projects, I have greatly benefited from the fruitful exchanges with numerous members of Bahtera and Teraju, internet listservs of worldwide translators of Indonesian and Malay, respectively. And, once again, I express my thanks to Ibu Wikan Satriati for her valuable assistance in both linguistic matters and liaising with the author. However, my greatest debt of gratitude goes to my friend and erstwhile fellow escort-interpreter in the United States Department of State International Visitor program, Mas Jojok Sumartojo of Atlanta, Georgia, who over many hours generously shared his thoughts on many linguistic aspects of this text.

I can only hope that my translation correctly reflects the insight and input from all these sources, and offer my sincere apologies where it has not.

And, once again I have been fortunate to have had as my copy-editor, Ms Diana Darling, resident of Ubud, Bali and author of the wondrous novel of that island, *The Painted Alphabet*.

Finally, I am deeply grateful to my wife, Scholastica Auyong, who makes all things possible in my life and whose presence reminds me every day of my abiding love for Southeast Asia.

Glossary

adat (Ar) all the differing unwritten traditional laws, rules, and norms governing societal interaction and behavior within the various ethnic and tribal groups throughout Indonesia and Malaysia.

adat besara dispute adjudication by the *kampung*'s team of adat law experts. Adat law and norms are believed to have been handed down by the authority of adat law in the eighth layer of heaven.

antang an heirloom earthenware jug (*guci kuno*). Accumulating these is viewed as a sign of one's growing wealth.

balai-balai 1) a platform, about half a meter above the ground, made especially for a part of the ceremony being held outside the longhouse. At the *balai-balai*, a special ceremony calls down certain gods and goddesses not yet involved in the ceremony. The special ceremony held here sometimes takes up to three days and nights; 2) a kind of temporary sitting arrangement (*kursi sementara*) made from yellow bamboo, where newly arrived guests are received in a form of ritualized welcome, whereby they may be smeared with plain flour and prayed over to free them from all misfortune and danger, and then cleansed with water in a manner prescribed by adat.

baley tota a bathing *balai-balai*. See (2) of *balai-balai* above.

balian means both the shaman / healer (*dukun* in Indonesian) and the ceremony he or she (there are female *balian*) performs or assists in.

bekantan the proboscis monkey. With its image of reddish-brown colored fur and absurdly long nose, *bekantan* is also a disparaging term for Westerners.

belontang carved post of ironwood used to tether the sacrificial water buffalo in the *kewangkey* ceremony.

berahan when, after rice planting is completed, the village men go into the forest to gather forest produce to sell in the larger populated areas or to middlemen.

bilik the side-by-side apartments that each contain a family unit within the longhouse.

bulé (Jav) Literally, albino. Now a common derisive term throughout Indonesia for white Westerners. See also *bekantan*.

dempak low-lying croplands, vulnerable to frequent flooding, but gaining much soil nutrients from that.

domek funeral dirges of the *kewangkey* ceremony.

gantar dance held on happy occasions. Gantar means a joint of bamboo filled with gravel or kernels of corn and whose ends have been plugged by wood. The right hand shakes the gantar to create a certain rhythm of sound while the left hand holds a stick.

huma land cleared by the slash-and-burn method for hill-rice cultivation.

jamban a floating platform made of logs secured to the riverbank by rope, rattan or cable that can be let out or drawn in according to the height of the river. It is where boats come to moor, people bathe and wash clothes, and often includes a closed and roofed outhouse.

jatilan one of the traditional possession dances of Java, this one involving a plaited bamboo hobbyhorse.

Kakak/Kak generally, older sibling, and here mostly older brother. Besides being the normal kinship term, older brother is also

one of intimate endearment used by a girl for her male
sweetheart. Similarly, *Adik* (younger sibling), and here little
sister, is how *Kakak* would address his girlfriend.

kampung general term for either a rural or urban village.

kangkung Ipomoea aquatica, commonly called water spinach, a
highly nutritious tropical semi-aquatic leaf vegetable, widely
used in Southeast Asian cooking.

kewangkey the secondary burial ritual of the Benuaq Dayak,
whereby the bones or any other remains of the deceased
are removed from a temporary resting place and placed in a
hanging coffin called a *tempelaq*. The purpose of completing
the various kinds of secondary burial among the Dayak
is for the souls of the departed to achieve a peaceful and
glorified state in the afterlife.

kris   the wavy stabbing knife of the Malay world, ritually forged
and hence with mystical powers.

ladder of gold a literal translation of *tukar bulau* in the text. It
is where the deities descend to earth during the healing
ceremony. Their appearance on the tukar bulau seems to
precipitate its own ceremony.

Letala the higher essence; the deity who lowered humanity to
earth from Lumut.

Lumut According to the Benuaq ethnic group of Dayak in East
Kalimantan and the group central to *Ceremony*, Heaven is
at the top of Mount Lumut, which is located on the border
between East and Central Kalimantan.

lungun the hollowed-out tree trunk serving as a preliminary coffin
for the departed family member.

ngayau from the verb *kayau*, to decapitate, behead and the word
widely used for the ritual headhunting of the intertribal wars
and feuding that wound down after the Dutch-sponsored

"Peace Meeting" at Tumbang Anoi, Central Kalimantan, in 1894.

ompong a status ritual of the Benuaq Dayak involving the conferring of personal obligation in exchange for the acceptance of a gift; the more ancient and valuable the gift, the heavier the burden of obligation to the acceptor.

peles a ritualized placatory offering to the gods.

*perahu*a general term for boats and watercraft other than rafts.

tengkawang Kalimantan people use the buttery seed or nut oil from the tengkawang tree for frying and medicines. Indonesia is the main exporter of tengkawang products widely used as substitutes for cocoa butter in chocolate, and for wax, cosmetics, pharmaceuticals, soap, margarine, and grease.

salung visitors from other villages or longhouses, invited for a special reason, such as witnessing a ceremony.

selampit a length of rattan that tethers the sacrificial water buffalo to the belontang carved post.

serapo a kind of *balai-balai*-like structure up to about 100 meters in length and roofed over with *rumbia* (sago) fronds. The serapo is constructed to accommodate visitors when ceremonies are performed.

tempelaq a hanging coffin for the bones of the deceased in the final stage of the *kewangkey* ceremony.

*tinting*red sticky rice, cooked by steaming in a section of young bamboo.

tiwah another kind of Dayak secondary burial ritual, this one performed by the Ngaju Dayak of Central Kalimantan. Similar to *kewangkey* of the Benuaq. In this novel, the author uses the terms synonymously .

Tuan sir. Often used when addressing or speaking about a European or Western male.

tujang a boat-shaped object with imagined flying powers used in the *balian* ceremony to search for the lost or abducted soul of a sick person.

Ceremony

I

Climbing Mount Lumut:
Ascending To Heaven

1

Like suddenly awakening from deep sleep. Heavy, every part of me. My hands, my feet, everything stiff when I moved them. No energy at all. My heart throbbing. My breathing ragged. I could sense it.

In my ears, the rumbling and thundering of pounded music. A jingling of hand bells and metal bracelets, soft singing of the *balian bawo*—the healer—and, right beside me, mournful sobbing. All of this seemed to have dragged me from the depths of sleep where a most astounding dream had been underway.

I opened my eyes, heavy under a cloud of drowsiness still hovering over me. I glimpsed a flash of the morning through the lattice of the longhouse wall and heard the clucking and crowing of the chickens outside. Oh, right—had to be my Speckle crowing in his cage, something I had not heard since I was last awake, a long time ago. I knew that he had served me the most.

I noticed traces of her sobbing on Mother's face. Father's face, the faces of family members—naturally I recognized them all—surrounded me. I caught the grief-colored flecks of light radiating from their looks. A question silently lodged in me. What secret was hidden in each one of those faces? Was this a reunion after my far-off wanderings? Or had something really unusual happened here beyond my knowing?

Uncle Tunding was still caught up in his balian dance on the longhouse veranda. The music of the *kendang* drum and the gongs accompanied the balian dance, along with the ritual language now reaching its end. The rattan floor twitched and creaked beneath the rough-stitched *jaliq* mat as Uncle Tunding swayed and swung his dance toward me, bearing pieces of finely shredded banana leaf.

These shredded leaves called *selolo*, thought to possess mystically therapeutic power, were in the balian's right hand, while the *getang*, musical metal bracelets, spoke most harmoniously in rhythm with all the sounds being struck.

The wet forest wind pierced the cold morning fog, biting through the cracks and gaps in the floor. Most of the rattan strips were stained from now dried sirih leaf spit. Meanwhile, I was laid out on a mat of fine, shiny *sega* cane eight hand spans in length that held special meaning in critical moments, particularly for sick people or women about to give birth.

Thinned down, I felt, all wrapped in a blanket woven by Mother from *kerop* root fibers and rarely used, unless for a big feast or when undertaking long and dangerous travel.

Near the corner of the room flickered the fading pale resin flame. A few rosined sticks burned feebly on the veranda. My eyes fastened on the ironwood pillars of the longhouse upon which were nailed the heads of various kinds of deer with their branching antlers. Also up there were the horns of water buffalo and wild cattle, attached to other pillars. From those horns and antlers dangled various kinds of swords in their sheaths on which were carved scenes and animal images. Below the ceiling hung racks of plaited bamboo for holding spears and other weapons of war.

The sharp yipping of dogs, the snuffling and snorting of pigs mingled underneath the longhouse. Unclear voices sounded in the *bilik* on either side of us. A disorderly line of a few human heads faded away down the veranda until it reached the door, where hung baskets of offerings for the bad spirits, with bananas and pinang nuts still in bunches. The door was entirely fringed with gorgeously colored young coconut fronds. Over to the right hung the flowers of a *nibung* palm, and coconut flowers burst forth from their sheaths. In the middle of the veranda hung flowers together with the requisites for the "ladder of gold" ceremony. The materials were piddling and trivial, merely boughs of betel fronds dangling among banana stems and surrounded by copper salvers brimming with various sorts of festive foods.

A set of musical instruments was being played somewhere else—a fact proclaiming that the night before, maybe even for several nights before, a grand *balian* feast had taken place. And in the midst of such merriment I felt like an outsider.

Abruptly, my eyes fell upon Mother's swollen face. Joy and elation danced in the gleam of her eyes. Her smile, cool with contentment, looked splashed across her handsome face, even though scars of the suffering kept buried within her still clearly lingered there.

Her motherly stroking my disheveled hair seemed increasingly to conceal a secret I couldn't understand. And that secret was all the more impenetrably hidden from me when suddenly she broke into fits of sobbing as she hugged my still trembling body.

"God! God! Oh Divine One! My child, my child! Oh, thank you! Thank you... God! My child! Oh, departed soul, Divine One. Thank you! Thank you! Thank you...!"

Her tears poured out. As if a heavy burden had fallen from her shoulders together with the choked sobbing and dripping tears, shackling me with ignorance of what had happened. Because I knew everything about the kind of person my mother was. A woman full of affection and love and self-sacrifice whom I revered with all my heart, a gentle-souled mother, but one who'd stand firm against any blows. Enthroned in her soul was a refinement noble but intangible, except to the sensitivity of someone closest to her—the drops of her blood.

Mother let go of me and raised her face from my body when Uncle Tunding squatted beside me. The *getang* on his wrists clinked and jingled as he brushed the shredded banana leaves across my face. Then lowered these to my chest. There was a coolness in the touch of these fibers, the caressing of a wanton breeze.

Only now did I realize that this balian ceremony was for me. What I didn't understand was why I felt in perfect health. But realizing the sumptuousness of the offerings, I knew that the patient now undergoing such a ritual must have arrived at the most critical stage. I couldn't care less! Instinctively, I shut my eyes tight as Uncle Tunding brought his final incantations to an end.

Let's get this over and done with, now that another event is blocking my inner vision, roughly forcing my mind to bring to light that strange and truly wondrous event. A repetition zoomed in from some occult distance and extended across a landscape of events, down long and astonishingly colored memories. A silent movement from the experiences of adventure seemed to reveal itself from the depths of a well of unexpected meanings.

2

Suddenly, I am in the midst of a vast field of flowers. My feet tread a trail that stretches straight ahead, almost beyond the horizon. The right and left of the trail is overgrown with a luxuriance of moss, alive, and spreads out like a green mat or rug. The desolate loneliness welling up in every direction creates silent residences in every tree, in lofty stands of bamboo.

Flowers waft their soft aromas, as the leaves, bending under the weight of dew drops, glitter in the light of the far-off sun. An unearthly dance seems to float over the rushing stream of events, an obscurity spreading across the heavens. Like a mooring post of a river landing on a glorious morning. A dance of intoxicating colors, born and emerging from frame after frame of a vast canvas, forming paintings of events in time, in one space after the other. Violet replaced by orange red, which then appears purple and blue, yellow, red, light red and sea green. Then, thousands of colors unite in compositions of charm and enchantment. A most appealing impression of the change of scenes, dream-like and delighting. As if I'm standing on a perfect height and all kinds of scenic views have readied themselves for me to be enticed by fantasies, spiritual compositions without end.

A terrible speed on wings of adventure, like those of spirits or gods, carries me to a destination dense with enigma. A fresh and astounding journey for me, where at every stop there is always some heart-pounding test. The irrational curiosity that drags me forward at such high speed is also a secret kept from me, a giant power which I have never before possessed.

The first thing I become aware of is my speckled rooster. It is still gripped in my left hand since I had taken him from its cage. There is a little bit of a commotion with Mother. When I say good-by to her, she keeps forbidding me to go. But I force myself free of her embrace.

"Grandpa is waiting out front!" I snap at her. "He's asked me to go to Grandma's home," I say as I roughly wrench myself free. I see her stunned look, her eyes filled with pity and compassion for me. But I hurry away, not caring.

I walk out onto the veranda. Behind, I hear Mother's pitiful sobbing. I feel some regret at hurting her. But I can't hold back my eagerness to leave any longer. My longing to see Grandma mysteriously pulls me into a state of a blazing urgency. Especially as Mother has been able to frustrate every plan I have ever made.

I arrive at the open ground where two mortars are lying quietly overturned on the ground. Bran, scattered all over the place, with some of it piled beneath the mortars. Several pounders have been set standing on end at the edge of the yard. This is where the women of the longhouse usually pound the paddy or make rice flour.

The longhouse has only one stairway. Made of ironwood. Planed smooth, it has as many hewn notched steps as are needed to reach the floor of the longhouse. On both sides a sort of railing has been set up to serve as wooden handholds. The wood is smooth and dull-colored from being constantly handled by so many people.

I reach the ladder now laying face down, turn it face up, and descend as I hold onto the railings now slippery from the dew. Grandpa greets me with a smile. That smile is special, one that I had known in the past. Yes, that happened way long ago and is only now reappearing.

It isn't only his hair, but everything about Grandpa looks as if it is getting whiter. Still, a lovely merriment hangs about his smiling face, a face that enthrones authority and power. It is just then that I recall Father. The mournful face that released me minutes ago is one half of the smiling face in front of me now.

The yard is quite wide and as long as the longhouse itself. To its east, a trail winds down to the river. There sampans and *perahu* are moored to a *jamban*, a platform of floating logs secured to the riverbank .

To the west of the yard is a heap of firewood. Used tools of the balian and strips of rags are drying in the sunlight on a line of twisted rattan. Nearby is a dying bonfire from which puffs of smoke are still rising. Off to the side, a few dogs are lying on the ground. Further to the west, cane scrapers are bound up, and far beyond the yard, rattan is spread out to dry. Rattan and cane scraped clean of their outer skins whitening on top of drying racks.

In the space underneath the longhouse, pigs are wandering about or wallowing in a pen smeared black with slime. Chicken cages dangle here and there on wood strips fastened to adjoining pillars of the longhouse. Several cages for parrots cages and other kinds of birds are suspended indifferently on the building walls. These also hold the sort of parakeets called *pialing* and *teriep*. The wall is made from tree bark. Gloomy and dark in color. Split and dirty here and there. An unpleasant odor piercingly assaults me. Just like some scared kid from somewhere else, I reflexively grab hold onto Grandpa's hand.

"I've heard the death bird, the *sentapit*, sing seven times," he says. "The sign I would come for you. Your mother and Uncle Tunding stirred up a storm. I almost couldn't meet you again this time. Luckily, everything got straightened out."

"Yeah," I say, "Mother is really fussy. She didn't want me to go."

Again, Grandpa smiles.

Morning has descended upon the world. Mingling and merging voices and sounds.

The two of us head north.

3

The longhouse behind us stands decrepit and surrounded by fruit gardens of all sorts, relics of Grandpa and Grandma. All around the longhouse tower coconut trees and, under these, shady coffee bushes. The aroma of the coffee berries seeps into our noses. Elsewhere, the rottenness of durian flowers squish, like when you step on spit. All the fruit trees are in full blossom.

The forest we are making our way through is *belukar*, secondary growth, the remains of dry-field farming that had once been here and now has shifted elsewhere. The further in we go, the younger the forest is, a sign that every year the people of the longhouses are moving their fields to places farther and farther away.

We arrive at the newly cleared cropland we call *huma*. Logs and giant stumps scorched black lie on the ground, mobbed by bushes and other wild growth. Sometimes there are the leafy clusters of pineapple plants, papaya and banana trees, and wild yams and other forest tubers. Everything is growing wild and uncared for and the grass is getting high. The excrement of polecats and bird droppings are spattered and piled everywhere.

The more marshy areas are dense with taro, and stalks of *kangkung* creep about with total freedom. The posts of the little raised granaries still filled with paddy are stuck in the higher huma land. Cassava stalks and clumps of sugar cane with their whitening flowers stand luxuriantly erect. We pass by the watch hut on the newest huma. Some pet birds chitter in their cages hanging on its outer walls. As we proceed westward, the road descends and ends at a bamboo water pipe. Its water has been dammed below it, resulting in a kind of little fish pond. The water is clear and we can clearly see a few fish swimming about. All along the edge of the pond formed by the little stream is the fish-poison plant. I once used that plant to stun fish in the pond and, for that, earned a few good ear tugs from Mother.

This is the last of the clearings. At its edge stands the dense forest. We enter it and come across a brook where fish traps have been set on its banks. A wooden footbridge stretches across, old and weathered. We come to a slightly raised stretch of land where great *jengan* trees tower overhead. People use these trees to catch birds. A tree would be pruned to release its sap, and decoy birds would call their fellows to alight there and then be stuck in the sap.

Elsewhere there is a vast and shady banyan tree as thick with birds as with its leaves. They have come to perch here because its fruit is ripe. Together with Tingang, I often spread birdlime to catch hornbills, quail, parrots, and whatever else ill-fated enough to be caught by our sticky traps. It's something quite fascinating to do.

Farther on in is a little track made by forest animals. This track is tightly hemmed in by the steep sides of a ravine. There *poti* and *sungaq* snares of bamboo are set. These are very dangerous, and pigs, deer, wild cows, and even rhinos often fall prey to them.

At the foot of the ravine, traps are set at the holes that gape around the hill. With luck these bristly traps often catch porcupines whose stomachs contain bezoars. Such talismans are aggressively competed for by the Chinese who come from the towns.

A little to the east of this streamside is a stretch of low land that begins alongside a great river that flows far downstream to the south. Often during the flood season here, bamboo fishnets called *kalak* are set up, their mouths facing the source and flow of the current. In the dry season, the bends in this river hold lots of milkfish, and also mackerel, our dolphin-like *ikan patin*, and *ikan baung*, often called pike. Kampung people like to catch these dim-witted creatures with hooks baited with just slices of raw cassava.

It is during the hot seasons that the crocodiles and turtles normally lay their eggs. The crocodiles are the stupider of the two. Their eggs are left in a mess of leaves and sand between the broad roots of trees fairly far inland. Their undersides leave a trail in the mud and sand that's easy to recognize, and the kampung folk who discover this happily place the eggs into their rattan *anjat* baskets. By contrast, the turtles only lay their eggs in the sand of the riverside beaches and don't sit on them until they hatch. Thus, it's harder to find their tracks, and, especially if these have been swept away by the dew or drizzly rain, the searchers will lose sight of them.

These eggs in shallow sandy holes, if not carried off by floods or taken by people or devoured by egg-eating animals, hatch by themselves. A fascinating sight, when hundreds of these turtle children crawl along searching for the river's edge. Those that do not bump into snakes, jackals, or otters along the way, will safely begin their new lives, a thing both delicate and difficult.

An odd journey, I think. A wordless pace has brought us to all the places my feet have once touched. After passing several lakes, rubber plantations, fruit orchards, groves of sago, nipa, and sugar palm, bamboo thickets, and a few plots of cropland, we finally arrive back at the grounds of our longhouse.

"A beginning of the journey for you," says Grandpa suddenly. "Gaze for the last time upon everything that you have enjoyed here. A distance will stretch out between you and worldly goings-on. The eternal and the perishable—the two totally opposing poles. Here is where you head toward the everlasting."

I am silent, not understanding.

"This event will soon become clear to you, my only grandson. Beloved soul," and here Grandpa looks at me penetratingly, "you are now eighteen years old, the most sensitive and complicated age, according to our adat. You are aware that a son is the pillar of the longhouse, the sacred decapitating blade, the blowpipe and the steel shield, and at certain times he is the arrow swift as lightening hunting its prey. But remember, too, that he is the gentle heart that loves, is the unity of the knitted threads of the net that gathers a clan." Grandpa sniffs softly.

I remain silent, understanding less and less.

"You have passed a difficult time. But what happened is just the beginning. Very soon you will clearly see another reality behind the reality of your senses. Therefore, gaze to your heart's content for the last time, for such a moment will soon pass."

I feel strange, but Grandpa immediately reads my thoughts.

"Yes, the beginning *is* strange. But a true man is always able to overcome obstacles. This is the road." He points. "Go alone. We will soon meet in a place not in this world. Be off now!"

And, just like that, Grandpa himself disappears, like a wisp of smoke billowing into a chain of clouds in its ever-recreating composition.

A weird kind of force pushes me on my way. A strip of road suddenly appears and stretches out before me. I never before bothered to wonder just where that road reached its end. In a city, out in some territory, or far-off kampung? My feet move forward as if all that could be wished for depends on them, nor do they want to stop. A fearful pace takes me farther and farther into the unknown and unknowable.

The long and deserted road brings me abruptly to the riverbank. As I descend towards the edge of the water, a middle-aged man greets me. He has stunted arms and a gimpy leg. He's also wall-eyed, and his earlobes are broad and hang loosely, like an elephant's. Fat lips and a head that is completely bald and bumpy. He keeps nodding attentively and greets me with a sinister smile.

"I've been waiting for you for a while now. Our envoy told us of your coming." His lips open and shut in a funny way as he speaks.

His hand shakes and jiggles a blowpipe. A tube holding the blowpipe's darts—its "children"— gapes open, hanging smartly at the man's waist.

"Here's the boat," he says harshly. "You've got to cross over by yourself. If you overturn or come back here, this blowpipe's children will end your tale."

I don't dispute this and just take the paddle. But damn it all! The sampan seems to be leaking. Water is coming in fast. When I am about to say something, the man's pitiless glare bores into me. What else can I do? I jump into the sampan and immediately dig the paddle into the water. The sampan races against the current as I busily bail out the water pouring in.

The water of that river is strange, red like blood. The river itself is wide too, and makes me tremble there in the leaky sampan. To the right and left stand sheer walls of stone and rock. Far upstream I can hear a boisterous roaring, like a waterfall. Downstream is a blurred sparkling, almost right to the edge of the horizon, as if opening up onto a lake of immortality.

Almost without realizing it, I arrive safely on the other side of the river. Leap ashore. Odd! Here is that same fellow again, already waiting for me. With a sweet look and smile he offers a leaf to me. On the leaf is written a script and scratchings I don't understand. I accept the leaf and proceed onward.

After a steep climb, I hit flat land. All about stand trees that seem to be mumbling or grumbling a greeting to this solitary stranger. I pay no attention, and walk straight on until my way is blocked by a large fallen tree trunk. It is very long, so long that I can't tell where its roots start and where its crown ends. Strange! When I try to leap over it, there is a lightness to my body and I land right up on its top, a height three times my own. Then I leap down to the other side. And again, strangely, there is someone else awaiting me. He too has physical defects, like the watchman at the river that I met earlier.

A leaf is held out to me. A leaf with writing on it. He smiles to himself and I walk on.

I pass through ninety-seven obstacles, some of them horrifying. A big python hisses when I have to walk in front of it. A bear, a lion, a tiger, an orangutan, several crocodiles and lizards. Packs of jackals, flocks of crows, carrion-eaters and other savage animals that have been waiting in certain places. And there are a number of other things that hinder my steps, so that the final ones, the climbing and descending, are full of heart-stopping perils. I have to clamber over a steep hill of sharp rocks. When I reach the crest, I see an expanse of very fine plantation land way off in the distance. But everything is still hazy because of the distance, which challenges the pace of my travel.

Almost everything I see is in gray.

4

The gentle fragrance of flowers abruptly hardens into a slap of rot. I seem to be walking on piles of carrion whose pools of decaying stench thicken in the air. So quickly everything now arouses loathsome and nauseating feelings. The panorama wobbles and sways with the sudden appearance of a frightful dance, as if a million giants and demons have emerged from behind the silent stands of trees and bamboo. I sense Death lurking with my every step and standing guard with its million occult claws.

Secret supernatural hands are what can save me. I feel myself staggering and choking on the rotten stench of the root poison. As I step beyond the perimeter of the planted area, a man greets me. And just like the other ninety-seven people I have encountered so far, this fellow too has creepy physical abnormalities.

But this isn't the moment for examinations. I don't have time to study him closely, let alone laugh, for the man at once steadies my tottering body. Wipes my nose with his handkerchief. An odd and pleasing aroma emanates from the handkerchief and immediately revives my strength.

"Only two more tests for you…" The fellow has a comic way of mumbling. I stare at him, planting a question mark before him.

"You will very soon enter into a new life without equal!" His voice sounds like the squawking of a drunken magpie.

I nod without understanding. I want to hurry off again. But the fellow's hand holds me back. "Here is the ninety-eighth letter for you. May you stay safe." His mumbling mouth and his tightly shut eyes make him look prayerful and add a strangeness to his funny looks. He slaps my back.

"Get going!"

The path gradually broadens and the journey grows more pleasant since I don't have to climb any more mountains or clamber down any more river valleys and ravines. The farther I go, the more I feel throbbing life waiting to greet me off in the distance. Like a quiet beckoning calling softly from beyond view. Like the excited pounding in the chests of lovers trying out love. I keep moving into that distance.

Now my vision has gotten confused. A disgusting sight hems me in everywhere. Filthy, miserable houses are planted on both sides of the way. This settlement surrounds a strong fortress. Houses stand in an orderly line, the barracks old and crumbling, and shabby huts are shaky to the point of collapse. A sight that saddens me. The depth of its utter poverty is heartrending. This kampung seems to have been sunbaked year after year, until its life's breath has grown feeble and dry.

There is a pitiful and pathetic look to life here. The people are dressed in rags. They are unkempt and dirty. Worry and suffering leave deep grooves on their faces. They stagger as though fierce combat with evil giants has left them exhausted and squeezed dry. Suffering is ravaging this group of human beings, clawing and tearing them apart without pity.

What a contrast from the majestic fortress that stands amidst the kampung! The common people are no more than pictures of the walking dead, a coffle of slaves in an underground mine, herded out by their overseer to absorb the sun's rays and drink in the open air.

I now stand before the gate, the mouth of that fortress. A chilling sight stops me in that archway. I stare, stunned, at two horrible deadly smacking tongues. Suddenly someone pinches my ear. I jump in surprise. *How rude can you be?* I think. But I stay quiet, resentment burning in my chest. Such an oppressive atmosphere, the air growing heavy and my throat dry. And the smile of this person, like the flash of a knife that just might plunge into my weary breast, astonishes me, paralyzes me from making the slightest move, and, as if enchanted, I nearly give myself up to my fate.

"Don't be afraid," says the fellow roughly. "This is the gate of life. Every person who passes through here will almost certainly taste eternal life. Beautiful happiness that knows no end!" His mouth stops babbling. Foamy spit speckles the corners of his lips.

A filthy sight, uninspiring and stupid, quite apart from the funny odd shape of his body.

"But this isn't your final obstacle. You, brother, surely witnessed the unappealing panorama out there. It is the punishment for transgressors. Some of them were lustful and wanted to be first, so they hurried to leave ahead of time. Others are the lazy ones, so they arrived very late. The gate was locked. Their reward is having to be satisfied with staying outside for a while." With a straightened forefinger, the man points to where the decrepit huts stick out of the ground. "What's important," he chatters on, "is that they have not yet been purified by their kinfolk, so that their right of entry is being held up. They've just got to accept this gloomy halt for a while." He appears to take a breath. His nose twitches comically as he makes a few quick snorts.

I wait.

The man stamps a command with his foot. At once, a bizarre troop of dwarves appear with a panoply of antique weapons. Some grip cudgels and spears, while others hold blowpipes, decapitating knives, axes, short swords, knives, numerous sharp-bladed weapons, while still others carry lengths of strong rope. Some of them brandish the *badik* knives of Makassar in one hand and cover their chests with shields. All are ready to lash out at their enemy.

It feels strange to be surrounded so swiftly by this armed band.

A signal from the first man makes my puny chest shake and tremble terribly. It seems this troop of dwarves are to escort me under guard through this archway. Two giant dragons wait ready to devour my little body. Their protruding tongues lick the air, and their eyes, red as *saga* berries, blink ferociously and hungrily. But the dwarves drive me ever closer to the snouts of these frightening wild beasts.

As the dwarves cheer, I feel that death has made its delicate way on every member of my body, has followed the course of every vein in my body and then stopped at my clot of a heart. Not one heartbeat more, the coldness of death rolls me up when the dragons lick my body, licking to devour me. Eyes shut, I feel I am between two jaws and the sharp fangs of the dragon are tearing my soft body to bits. I can feel the blood gushing out and splashing the mouths of the two ravening beasts. All this in the blink of an eye.

Strange. When I open my eyes, I am in front of a guard house. My heart is still beating and there isn't the slightest scratch on my skin. No dwarves, no dragons. A man stands there, the one from earlier, the first one.

Impudently, the man thrusts his hand into my pocket. Takes out the leaf I have brought with me since my first interception, considers it carefully, nods repeatedly, adds another leaf, puts it into my pocket, shakes my hand, bids farewell with high-sounding words, and then pushes me off on my way.

All so unexpectedly sudden. Like an intoxicating dream. I am stunned to view such grandeur towering before me. The fortress, so repulsive just minutes ago, is both gate and guardian of an inner dream palace.

The enchanting glitter and sparkle shoot off in rays of light from various angles of a unity of domes and the peaks of towers, like the sun with its multihued radiance. My undisturbed silhouette is clearly reflected on the marble floor I tread upon. Like a mirror lake, where the play of objects and celestial beings create the games of myriad moons, and stars and heavenly bodies play hide-and-go-seek in dim corners.

5

There seems to be an organized din greeting me from far off. There are the sounds of music being struck and the procession of songs. Its rhythm rises and falls in waves that billow and sway, sometimes calmly and sometimes hotly arousing.

There are, as well, cheers of joy and lively shouts creating a composition of exuberant manly tones. Sounds heave and pitch rhythmically in well-coordinated and beautiful harmony. This truly is the climax of the yearly feast that I know as *erau ngugu tahun*, the honoring of the Deity in return for all its blessings bestowed on us over the past year. A climax of gladness and delight.

Emotions, reason, and thought are practically powerless in such a situation. Because the background of events always drags and tugs with a will of its own.

The voices grow in unison. They dazzle me in a pure charm that is itself enraptured. Suddenly, twelve young people are standing before me. Their clothes are superb. Beautiful. Dazzling white. They come forward to greet me, smiling and nodding in respect. Behind them two white horses stand ready to pull a golden carriage.

"We are charged with greeting you, O Beloved Soul," says one of the youths. "The carriage is ready, the journey arranged to follow along the road of this City of Life."

"If all is in good order, the final test will soon begin," says another of them. Their faces have the all the innocence and good cheer of youth.

When I don't know what to do, all at once they lift me up and set me down in the gleaming carriage. The syce shakes the reins, and the horses take us around this astonishing city. Beauty truly beyond compare.

One of the youths politely explains to me the names, meanings, events, objects, the sights, inscriptions, buildings, and the streets we pass through. But the other youths always carefully keep their eyes on me, causing a clash within me between my annoyance and my awkwardly over-sensitive mind.

The panorama is overwhelming. Each object and vista possesses a mysterious charm. Holding and thrilling the visitors in their very souls. Like a mystical painting that slowly reveals itself from beyond the horizon, burnishing a dance of many hazy colors, that then become ever more clear, ever more clear, and finally give birth to a reality implanted right there before the eyes. A cycle of beauty, all different colors endlessly forming subtle and interlinking chains. Like a series of views in a gleaming dreamland.

The syce pulls back on the reins, and the golden carriage shudders and stops. In front stands a gate, thronged with people. The gate itself brilliantly adorned with all sorts of flowers and young coconut fronds dyed most colorfully. Swarms of other people mass around a little square field. The greenness the field has gone bare for several meters around. The air around it is very cool. The trees are heavily laden with fruits. So many kinds of fruit trees, so many!

Just inside the gate towers a building of extraordinary magnificence. It emanates a dazzling radiance. An extremely complex architectural form, refined, of genius that arouses fantastic ideas. A harmonious blend of materials, their mixed composition, and their placement on the building. The vertical sides, the spaces, the soft and hard colors and its spacious width and length, all pleasantly coordinated. The work of the talented architect gives rise to admiration and pleasure, the heart and soul soar, as if that building belongs to a long-lost age re-encountered today, and constitutes a palace to live in in the days of eternity yet to come.

I gape in amazement. I am barely aware of the first young man helping me down from the carriage. The eleven other youths arrange themselves on guard around the carriage, while two new ones dressed as attendants take my hand and lead me off. As if I were a war prisoner, or a criminal to be thrown into some dark keep.

But the atmosphere here is very different. The faces in the lively crowd are warm and friendly. Shouts of welcome, music and singing express a grandeur filled with love. The warmth of the greetings to a guest at the height of the feast glowing with love and affection. As when two majesties meet.

The great mob of people at the mouth of the alley suddenly parts. There now appears a middle-aged man together with his escort to greet me. The raiment of his exalted position glitters and sparkles in the light and is covered with ornament and badges of honor. A gleaming crown perches on his head, his trousers are gray, and on his feet gold slippers. From his fingers shine his rings, encrusted with sapphires and other gemstones. His step is spry, his face full of authority, and he extends his hand to me and smiles. We shake hands. He is carefree and gay. I myself stay silent.

"Everything has been recorded," the middle-aged man says, and stares at me. Smiling, his voice is deep at the start but shrill at the end. It resounds far, though rather hoarsely, and hits with force. "Let no one deny it. The feast is being held to welcome you. It's all joy and merriment here. For life is eternity itself. Only,"—and here the man peers sharply at me—"to receive you validly, you need the final test. You know this country, the Country of Heaven, the everlasting home of people who have won. Your cock must be pitted against our cock."

All of a sudden, I feel Speckle leap in the grip of my clasped arms.

"Eternal life's price is the spirit of earthly life. There's no cheating or scheming. Your soul cannot be helped if your cock loses. And there can be no bargaining over it. When you count off the hundredth leaf, that's spiritual eternity!"

The uproar of the spectators surrounds the square space. I brandish Speckle for all to see. He is ferocious in his eagerness, and thrashes and flaps about, keen to leap upon his opponent. The feathers of his neck bristle forward, his talons tear at the ground, his crowing bursts out shrilly from his long and slender throat. Nor is the other cock any less fierce. A doughty bird with a furious glare. As if to say, "I'm going to grind you into dust, you fool of a Speckle!"

Both cocks are ready to fight. Straining to be let loose. Strange! The one holding the cock of Heaven is my grandpa! My beloved grandpa, who a few moments earlier took me all around the longhouse neighborhood. An event the souls have to undergo when they are about to leave the earth.

Grandpa is silent. I am silent. No time to talk together, to say anything. The cockfight has to be reckoned with and the moment passes.

All around the edge of the arena is in uproar. In the middle of it, each cock probes for openings, ways to bring down his enemy. Back and forth they kick, back-swipe, and savagely peck. Every time the cock of Lumut pecks at my Speckle, thunderous shouting and cheering erupts, as if victory is within their grasp.

But of course Speckle is a brave and tough rooster. He never lets an opening get by him. When he pounces onto the breast of his enemy, his spurs catch the flesh under his opponent's wingpit. Little by little, blood flows. Spills onto the ground.

This wound doesn't weaken the fighting spirit of his rival. He is wild and fierce as any heathen warlord. His beak tears ferociously at Speckle's cockscomb. Speckle totters and bends weakly. The shrieks and yells of the onlookers grow all the more tumultuous.

I reel in despair. Speckle is being pressed harder and harder. He staggers and sways. He gasps and pants. His strength seems to steadily leave him, drained away by the blows of his redoubtable foe.

I think these are the final words of my life's story. My fate will be finished at the hands of the people of Lumut. Finished! Finished right here in this arena. I can't help him. To revive a new fighting spirit and strength in him is beyond me. The lunge of his foe sends Speckle sprawling in the middle of the arena, at which I almost shriek out!

But it looks like my Speckle has been granted a miracle. He rises up like a raging boxer, and leaps upon his enemy, pecking savagely at his eyes. As fast as lightning, his beak stabs the other's neck. A fierce blow, tearing right through the neck of the cock of Heaven. Against all expectations, his enemy collapses in the center of the arena, sprawling and gasping for the breath of life. But of course there is no life for him, no spirit of life! Finally, the bird is silent. Dead!

My cock, though, stands there in the middle of the cockpit with the air of a true winner. He's won! His crowing is ear-splitting.

I could never have imagined what happens next. A turbid atmosphere bears violently down on me. A ferocious wave of anger from the spectators billows and overflows, like the rolling and tumbling of terrible flood waters. Savage cursing and swearing, glares like wells of fire from the eyes of a million heads. Until the command, "Ge-e-e-e-t-t-t him!" from a middle-aged man makes me practically lose my senses and my balance too. I can't choose. Can't do it—my mind is paralyzed by the onslaught of the wave of wrath of the millions.

I snatch up Speckle from the arena, push through the raging mass, and dash off on flying feet. Keep running! Keep running! Run! Don't stop! Never stop! Behind me, though, comes the sound of pursuing feet. The sharp cries and brutish shouts thunder like the duel between two warriors of equal match.

I can do nothing else. Just run and run as fast as I can. I want to save my breath, this lowly soul. My most prized possession. I won't simply surrender it without doing something against those who would rob it from me.

But those malevolent shouts and yells are getting closer and closer. The nets of the chase spread to ambush me. The conical net of humans is shaping a trap. My ignorance of the region gives them an advantage as they close in to grab me.

The human wave can no longer be staved off. It is drawing ever closer and I realize that I am being cut off right in their midst. The well-executed encirclement snatches me up in a netting of angry human hands. Terror will shake the hearts of even heroes. Because the price of life depends on sighs and heartbeats that still throb and are free. Angry brutes will never spare it. They want life, blood and death!

And me? I feel I have hit absolute exhaustion. My body is like to crack apart, my joints all in agony, and helpless, without breath. An eternal silence seems to enshroud my body and take it to the black lands. Black, black, black! Everything goes totally black. Silent, cold and lonely.

I feel nothing anymore. Have I died…?

Dead…?

6

I felt the most extraordinary sense of ease when I opened my eyes again. An odd cheerfulness seemed to emerge from the vastness of space to brush my body with the water of life. I felt like I had just now laid down a heavy burden I carried from a distant adventure. A delicious fatigue remained and crept through every one of my joints, tickling and rousing my skin, shaking awake hope that was breaking like dawn. As if bringing me to a spring where my parching thirst could be quenched.

I saw that Uncle Tunding had been sitting on the longhouse veranda, beside the golden ladder. His chant had ended, and music was no longer being played. The crowing of roosters went on and on, and the barking of dogs competed with the snorting of the pigs. Each mouth spoke of some sad event, some extraordinary occurrence. Everything was all jumbled up. Empty whisperings. Screams and crying of babies. Guffawing young men just fooling around. The pounding of mortars. Giggling girls. The longhouse seemed now a messed-up concert stage. Within that gap of time, my eyes suddenly met Mother's eyes. She smiled as she stroked my head slowly. Beside her, Ifing, a pretty girl who often made me uneasy. Her adolescence had blossomed in perfection. And now her wistful eyes gazed at me.

"I'll tell you about an amazing experience," I said haltingly. I still felt short of breath. Ifing still stared at me wide-eyed, never looking away.

Father smiled. Mother had stopped crying.

The morning smiled sweetly.

II

Balian: The Healer And The Ceremony

1

A longhouse, the home of many people, consists of several dozen rooms with dozens of family heads. Some longhouses might hold hundreds or even thousands of people. This is because a village generally has only one house, that being the longhouse. However, the people are always procreating, making the longhouse with its limited space always noisy and crowded. This communal lifestyle, handed down through the preceding generations, strengthens the tradition of loyal togetherness. As the pioneers in the founding of a village—or more precisely the construction of the longhouse— were originally from just one family, this family flourished and produced their descendants who then just kept on living in the longhouse as the years and generations passed. Naturally, it is hard for them to go off and live apart, especially given the factors of blood, *adat* law and customs, belief, livelihood, the limits of their knowledge, and so forth. A strong bond makes it possible for the longhouse to keep them there in stable circumstances.

A thing closed in and dark.

I myself was born and raised in the life of the longhouse. Of course, I was familiar with the ins and outs of life and living in this form of togetherness and knew these very well, even intricate and precise matters, within which one often encountered oddities that I was not quite able to accept wholeheartedly. It was the same as when I couldn't analyze and explain something with reason in any clear and definite way. I felt this cycle was only devotional. Constant rituals… dragging along through ceremony after ceremony. The journey of life in a long and far-reaching cycle that I could not avoid because my presence there demanded compliance.

2

The *balian,* or healing, ceremony was being prepared even though
the harvest had somewhat deteriorated. The price for the fruit of
the *tengkawang* tree was less than satisfactory. Uncle Teau had just
come back with the receipts from the sale of resin and rattan. The
price of rubber and coffee had fallen a lot this year.

"Those damned Chinese!" said Uncle Teau peevishly. "Always
the crop prices keep changing." He sounded funny saying this.
Then, picking up the thread, his wife, Bibi Rayan, rattled on,
grumbling and nagging, "They've got some nerve... we upriver
people are the stupid ones. Always getting tricked."

This sort of news jumps rapidly from mouth to mouth. Forms
chorus upon chorus that go on and on, seasoned and spiced,
considered and re-considered in witty and comical thoughts and
ways. Then, it's gone, gone with the wind. And the longhouse folk
go back to their busy daily lives.

The sounds of the pounder hitting the mortar never stopped.
Girls were pounding paddy. Other girls made rice flour. A few people
split wood in the open space around the longhouse. Off and on,
thudding sounds emanated from the side of the building. Probably
youths plucking coconuts and letting them drop to the ground.
The shrieks and yells of children sounded off in the distance. The
sounds of flute and drum blended. There was a rhythmless beating
on the bronze kettles and iron gongs. Little kids banging away,
just having fun. People coughed and sneezed. During the days in
preparation for the healing ceremony, the longhouse was busy, with
a lively and cheery atmosphere.

The longhouse elders decided in council to perform a healing
ritual, a balian, for the safety of my soul. I myself could do nothing,
even though when it came to belief, I was actually more of a denier.

Nonetheless, the facts speak for themselves. Little by little, I recovered from the grave sickness that almost ended my young life. It had laid me low for a long time, wilted and withered, and just about extinguished the light of my dreams, desires and my life in the days to come.

The *senteau* ritual of clairvoyance that searches for the cause of sickness, was held the day before yesterday. But the results weren't very convincing. Uncle Jomoq saw only vague images in the senteau mirror. At a quick glance, there appeared only a blackish dot that occasionally fluttered about like an old and frail moth. But even after scrutiny, it became harder and harder to determine the shape of this image, as it moved about, upside down, distant and faint. For almost an hour, Uncle Jomoq wrestled with that indistinct figure, studied it, analyzed it, guessed at its exact meaning and significance. So far, he hadn't been able to determine the cause of the sickness from all the signs, so the search was halted. He was still feeling out of sorts when he blew out the candles, sprinkled yellow grains of raw rice, folded the "cloth of mirrors" and extinguished the incense burner. Without a word, he lay down on the ground at an angle away from his now-snoring wife. His thoughts were still full of the strange shadows in the ritual mirror.

Also difficult to interpret was another obscure shadow behind the first one. That other image sometimes moved to the left and the right of the first one, and sometimes to the front and sometimes to the back of it. It was hard to guess its shape. Studying it closely made it slowly move away, leaving a fretwork of scratches on the first image. Sometimes it seemed to be stabbing with a *kris*, sometimes seeming to raise a black hand to lash out with a whip. And, then again, swaying and twisting from side to side like a possessed dancer in the middle of the arena, striking out here and there like in *jatilan*, with its demonically possessed dancer astride his plaited bamboo horse. Then the image changed into a horrifying masked performance, pouncing right and left, and savagely beating the first shadow. And when Uncle Jomoq decided to halt this clairvoyance, he vaguely made out the second image dragging the first one to a wide-yawning chasm. The man's heart throbbed and he took a long breath.

He closed his eyes. Tried to sleep!

His head felt very, very heavy.

3

"I've found the key," said Uncle Jomoq with complete certainty. The elders who had consulted together this morning sat face to face. Waited for the old healer, the most trusted in the kampung, to continue. He said earnestly, "We've got to conduct the ceremony in search of the soul immediately."

Uncle Jomoq then related his strange experience the previous night after completing the *senteau* ceremony. He had found himself walking all alone through a deserted kampung. The houses were lined up very nicely, neatly planned and built in a uniform style, and standing all along the straight kampung road. The road itself was bordered by thick and soft-leaved *beluntas* bushes trimmed chest-high. Very silent, the road was, with not a person outside any of the houses. And then he arrived where the road ended at a very odd-looking house. This house too was quiet, with not a sound of life's heartbeats.

At the front of the house was a yard with round pillars. These were carved with old-fashioned patterns in colors that were old and faded. Here and there hung decorations with striking colors. At its very front was affixed a ladder made from a kind of black wood. Its color too was old and worn-out. On the right and left of the ladder sat two dogs, their tongues sticking out.

The house was built in the form of a "stage" house, that is, one built on stilts. High and trim. Its posts were blackening and stood in a regular alignment—a very fine building. It looked well cared for, only that it was very old, so that its original appearance had greatly faded.

Its walls were made of boards. These were decorated with carvings in the Lawangan style, that is, like the woodcarving of the Lawangan people who were the parent group of the little tribes in the interior. This parent group was long extinct, but its blood had dripped into the members of the little tribes that were its fragments.

The roof of the house was made of ironwood shingles. At the end of the ridgepole was a dragon, mouth agape. Painted very lifelike, eyes bulging, scales gleaming, and protruding tongue wrapped around a deer. The deer's head was dangling, eyes shut, and visage filled with terror. It was quiet all around, with no living radiance anywhere in the kampung. The two dogs were only statues, finely sculpted from clay. Pretty work.

The dense silence overflowed, clanged. Strange, there was something pale struggling beneath the house. Persistent! A chicken seemed to be flapping about, suffering awfully, shut up in an iron cage. A young cock. Its spurs barely grown, blunt. Its face was deathly pale, it fell flat, stumbled and dragged itself along, occasionally circling around feebly. Its head sometimes erect, more often mutely bearing its utterly painful suffering.

Uncle Jomoq moved forward to help the unfortunate animal. He was filled with pity and stepped towards the cage. But then, unexpectedly, a sudden strange voice resounded weirdly throughout the kampung. Many shapes and manners of voices broke out together. Rose in bizarre fusions and pooled in the air of the silent village.

Dogs barked, pigs snuffled and grunted, tigers growled. The whinnying of horses, the bellowing of water buffalo, the groaning of the sick, the chirruping of birds. There was a long scream. Long! All sorts of sounds clashed like fighting cocks. Each voice, each sound, banging and striking against the other.

The lonely kampung now suddenly filled with terrifying eeriness. And as Uncle Jomoq stood there bewildered by the hammering of this cacophony on his ear drums, an old, old man appeared standing in middle of the yard. With a voice both oppressive and sinister, he invited Uncle Jomoq up into the house.

This man was truly ancient. His hair was cotton-white, his chin whiskers were white and long. His mustaches lay fiercely athwart his face. His white eyebrows poked upward at an angle. Everything about him was the whiteness of old age. But his eyes gleamed sharply. White eyes! Like newly-sharpened spears. He was entirely white—but sturdy, as if age was unable to subdue his blood and flesh.

"I have been waiting for you for some time now!" The old fellow's voice sounded heavily from inside him. He invited Uncle Jomoq to sit in an old chair, the only one in the room. "You summoned me with no offering at all—that was entirely too presumptuous!"

He glared and continued, "Twice you have called me without a clear purpose! I could still control myself. And be patient! But with the third call, I can restrain myself no longer. You see that white fowl? I have taken it hostage. If by tomorrow I am not given offerings, I will kill that cock myself!" His voice suddenly pitched shrilly. Uncle Jomoq trembled.

"I hate the long-nosed, red-haired *bekantan.* They won't convert my grandson. I, Tonoy, will not have my offspring be led astray by bekantan!"

Uncle Jomoq was speechless.

"Remember!" the man continued, "If the offerings are not sent as quickly as you can, I'll cut that white cock's head off!"

"What offerings?" asked Uncle Jomoq, shaking.

"You're just like one of those outsiders. Remember, it can't be short of the least little thing. Including the pig's blood and liver cooked with sticky rice inside young bamboo! Forty kinds of offerings, all of different colors. And do not forget the water of the young yellow coconut. You have learned all the varieties of offerings and their ceremonies. Understand?" He drew in his breath. And gave a little cough.

Uncle Jomoq nodded. "Yes."

"Go home!" signaled his eyes. "You! Go back, I say!" rudely pointing his finger.

Uncle Jomoq was awoken by the strident crowing and squawking between the cocks and hens. Pigs and dogs fought with each other over the remains in the fire pit beneath the longhouse. It was a confused racket of voices.

He was slimy with sweat. His whole body was wet. His chest was still pounding. He mentally organized all the events that he had just experienced. How clearly that dream played out on his eyelids! Eight times that night he had been visited by the same dream. The spotless kampung, the old man, and the suffering white cock.

4

According to local belief, someone who has returned from Lumut shall be granted long life, many blessings and all sorts of good fortune. It would be a long time before Death could be brave enough to approach him after his name had been scratched off on the list of the occupants of the *bilik* on Lumut. He was one of those deniers, for his wild soul would not surrender to the spirits running Heaven. Take Grandpa Wowok, for example. He was over a hundred years old, his body was humped and bent, but he was still strong enough to go hunting and always had luck when he fished. The moment he hooked a big river fish, damned if that fish didn't get snapped up by a crocodile. Grandpa Wowok yelled, dragged along by a strong force. The kampung men were able to kill the croc, but Grandpa had almost fainted. The children cheered. "Grandpa Wowok, hunchie! Grandpa Wowok, widow man!" even though the truth was, he had never married in all his life.

I gave absolutely no thought to long life and plentiful blessings. Age and fortune depended on luck. Even the meaning of "coming back from Lumut" was still hazy. For me, it was only an odd experience, an event I had never before experienced. Was that really and truly Lumut, or only a *fata morgana*? For at the moment it occurred, I felt I was not whole. I was split between the spiritual me and the bodily me. Or was that what is called dying? Then what is the borderline between living and dying? Is it the moment the face pales and the breath is cut short? When the pulse beats no more? "No! No!" I was suddenly flustered by the sound of my own voice. It was all so complicated. I had no desire to pursue such metaphysical questions. Maybe I'd just better cut my own path ahead, open the door for my love—love that was always delayed.

"We have forgotten Tonoy, the god who forged and shaped the land." The voice of Uncle Jomoq broke the silence of the elders in middle of their deadlocked council. "He is angry about the unexpected events that have stricken our village recently."

"Of course, there are lots of things we can't avoid," said my father, continuing with this thought. "We are in the middle of a world that is wide open. So, like it or not, we too are open to all sorts of patterns of events and reality. Things involving time and place now have much changed. Including those *bekantan*. Must we go back to *ngayau* times, when we took heads?"

All of a sudden, I thought of Tuan Smith. The professor doing scientific research. What research, I didn't quite know. It wasn't too clear. Just reading, studying bones and human skeletons, it looked like. Checking and re-checking, measuring and weighing, kneading and squeezing, silently staring and lost in thought, and taking lots of photos. According to his friend, he was an anthropologist. All day long, this and that, then that and this! He just goes on wasting his time, occasionally bursts out into laughter, knits his brows, and compares pictures with the actual fossils. Thinking and thinking and making notes. A whole lot of them.

"Exposing the bones without making offerings to the spirits is surely an insult that goes beyond all bounds!" said Uncle Suto furiously. "There's never been any custom like that since our ancestors' time. If we living ones are angry, what about the spirits, who everyone knows are terrible and full of subtle forces?"

Tuan Smith insisted on carrying out research on the giant skeletons that are found in this region. There was much contradictory information about the cave-like graves at the head of the little river to the west of the kampung. Many of the skeletons had petrified. One of these was especially striking, a human skeleton of gigantic proportions. Its bones were huge and long and quite strange-looking.

That was the skeleton of Ayus, according to the stories of our elders. A hero, a hermit, a wise and righteous man, a savior. He possessed holy and magic powers, he was mighty in ages past, and never died. He has only fallen asleep, and at the right time will rise again and build a longhouse in a different shape. A reformer. Praised and honored by many. He was saintly and sacred. Many people went to his hermitage to ask for blessings. Set out offerings. Asked for salvation and sustenance.

But Tuan Smith didn't want to make offerings. He dared to hold these things in his hands and take photos. What's more, he even wanted to bring those fossils back to his country. No conclusions could yet be reached with any certainty. He said he needed time and absolute precision in order to verify his research.

"But what hurt the most was that Tuan Smith said that we need salvation—that we need a savior!" shouted Uncle Jomoq again. "He says we're still in shackles because we have no God."

In fact, Tuan Smith and two of his companions did show all sorts of pictures and slides, which, he said, were about the life of the Savior. The Redeemer who once had come to the world. The Bringer of Love. Who loved all creatures, but who had been crucified with bad men because of his philosophy which said, "If someone strikes your left cheek, give him your right one. If someone takes your shirt, give him your robe, too." His blood was spilled and it washed away the sins of man. The one who cleanses us of our sins! He arose from death because Death could not defeat him. He sits beside the Father in heaven. Watches over and gives deliverance to the community of his people.

I myself was not overly impressed by those glossy pieces of paper. There was nothing special about them except for pictures of a man with a high nose and gray hair. A child, a youth, and a grown man with a beard. Whom people always thronged around. Many people, even many soldiers. A silence, the muteness of pictures. Paper and dark images. Foreignness and non-understanding!

"I showed that foreigner that we have God," Uncle Jomoq continued. "Once with a crow. Once with a pigeon, and once with a hornbill. The man nodded, impressed."

Uncle Jomoq was known not only as an eloquent old man, he also had a good reputation as a balian. His pupils were spread far and wide throughout the other *kampung*. And his ability to show the foundation of our beliefs to Tuan Smith was an important part of his history as a healer. The results of his work were often too impenetrable for other healers to study.

His feet planted on the ground, Tuan Smith never blinked. The brilliant display of the crow. It made almost no sense. The crow, whose feathers were grayish-black, disappeared after swerving to bathe in a cloudbank. It flew far off. Got smaller and smaller, after veering and wheeling eight times over our heads.

The three foreigners stood alongside Uncle Jomoq. Crowds of spectators stood around the *balai-balai* structures following the ceremony. The foreigners, the obstinacy of Uncle Jomoq, and the question marks in their own hearts. The success or failure of the ceremony, the beliefs of the foreigners, and Tonoy? Would he come this time?

Confidently, Uncle Jomoq, as always, scattered yellow raw rice grains, uttered mantra, clapped his hands three times, then waved and called something far away. His face was filled with all the earnestness of an ascetic. His eyes were sharp, and his soul sank into a mysterious mood.

"He'll be coming very soon," said Uncle Jomoq. He pointed to the edge of the sky, the direction from which the crow would be coming. "His feathers are gray. Three times he'll circle around us, and then perch for a while on the top of that *nibung* palm. From there he will swoop down to the river in front of us, calling out three times before reaching the top of that cork tree, and from there he will finally return to heaven, which is called *jaun turu lepir*—the seven-layered cloud."

"What's his name?" asked Tuan Smith.

"Letala Senieng Jatu," replied Uncle Jomoq quickly, naming the god who had lowered humanity down from heaven.

And the crow did come. But its cawing was hoarse and strident, like someone sneezing. For a long time it watched the visitors, as if reluctant to come down to rest. It seemed to catch a foreignness greeting it on the ground. Looking at it.

Only its performance was unchanged, staying as it had been. Captivating swerves and gyres, prettily flapping wings, gliding and floating with charming allure.

A pigeon? Pretty to look at with its lovely feathers. Here he is. Yet another symbol, a procession new and strange for outsiders. Meeting the demands of curiosity. Rare performances hold many dangers, the space of a week being quite long for those with a thirst for entertainment. And there's not a thing here, dead quiet it is, with no movies!

The special swooping and swerving, the peculiar flapping of its wings, got the foreigners all worked up, asking that which could not be answered. *A pet? A bird of the croplands? In disguise or is it magic? The bird's not strange, there's a lot in zoos. A tropical bird. But how you make it come? Of course, with offerings, mantras and ceremonies!*

When it first appeared, it scored the foot of the western horizon. The clouds seemed wounded, the rainbow colors parted. It came close to the field, sheering off with graceful movements in response to Uncle Jomoq's request, at the wishes of the foreigners.

"He's another one of the gods?"

"Indeed, his name is Nayuq, from the eighth heaven. His hands grasp the fate of humankind."

The pigeon flapped four times and threw himself down on our heads. His feathers were clean, and his eyes… oh, his eyes! He was cautious. In his flying, in his swinging and swaying. He floated.

"With so many gods, doesn't rivalry arise among them?" Tuan Smith asked.

"Not at all. Because they have different places, positions, prestige, and powers. Like, for example, a government or military hierarchy. Each echelon has its own tasks and authority and rights."

"So, is there a High God?"

"Letala. He is the highest. The Creator."

"And beneath him?"

"Many, many. They are mentioned in the language of the healers, and given offerings, one after the other, and according to their ranking."

"And if, for example, the lower gods rebel against the highest god?"

"See, humans are always idealizing naïve thoughts. We always equate the instincts of the gods with the lusts of humans. Coups d'état never occur in heaven, because the gods do not possess lustful instincts."

"Heaven! What's that?"

"The house of eternity." Uncle Jomoq gazed deeply into the foreigner's eyes. They both looked at each other. The foreigner nodded.

"Is it like a palace, like a longhouse?"

"It is just like a kingdom. The highest god resides on Lumut as the center of heaven. The other gods occupy their places throughout the heavenly realm.

"And their subjects?"

"The spirits of people who win. The spirits of dead persons who were sent off to heaven in the *tiwah* and *kewangkey* ceremonies, their bones purified and put in their final resting place."

"And if those people had a lust for power?" persisted Tuan Smith.

"The world of the spirits is the one of immortality. All worldly instincts will have been cleansed. There are no physical cravings, because they went forward to greet the horizon of death. The inhabitants of Lumut exist in the world of life.".

"Including the underling gods?"

"All the citizens of heaven and their subjects."

"The signs of being convinced of the divine truth?"

"Maintaining contact, making dedications and offerings, and healing rituals."

"What if the supreme god becomes old, feeble, and dies?" Tuan Smith gave him no quarter.

"In heaven there is no old age. There's no counting the years or consideration of age. Not like here on earth. Everything is fixed in newness for all time. Because there is no death in that place."

"Surely its inhabitants get bored in such a fixed state."

"Bored? Haven't worldly appetites all been rooted out?"

"If so, there's nothing there."

"The tree of life is there."

"The tree of life?"

"Like our bodies. The heart beats, the breath moves in rhythm. All the members are bound together at the center of unity. The body is the heaven that appears in our eyes."

Uncle Jomoq smiled in satisfaction with his explanation. Tuan Smith and his companions kept nodding.

Had he and they been able to understand each other?

5

Oddly, my experience with women was an ordinary one that began with my being sleepy. I say ordinary, because Grandpa, then Father had the same kind of experience and then it fell on me.

Fell on me, I say, because that experience was like a lucky hit of a falling durian, in other words, I got something without trying. Something truly marvelous!

At the time, I was only fourteen years old. _Ompong_ was imposed on our village, that is to say, the ancient adat tradition that mostly was of a showy nature, the exhibition of wealth, goods and power. Kampung Utara had to do the work. Our longhouse was the _salung_, the first guests among all those invited. Seventy-five percent of residents attended for the sake of preserving our good name, displaying all their possessions and every insignificant little thing.

The ceremony was all joyous good cheer. A tiring journey, a full day's rowing. I fell asleep quickly. All jumbled up together in the longhouse rooms with lots of unfamiliar people. There was quite a large number of *salung*. Difficult to identify, what with many being foreign to our area, people face to face for the first time. Smiling or silent. A little laughter, or a huge uproar! A racket of many voices spilled swirling and washing throughout the longhouse.

I was awoken. Awoken by a softness that wedged up against me. Something pliant. Two sharply tapering hills that kept poking me. I was naïve. Strange! All of a sudden, everything got all stiff. I was a guest now, sleeping in a room under a mosquito net. The light was dim. I had no plans for women or girls. The suddenness was startling. Embraces, whispers, and tenderness that kept it standing. Tenderness or lust? Didn't push away, shifting, hands and embraces, a voyage over the waves that rose and fell, lulling something delightful. I journeyed on the surface of an arousing softness. It was unbearable, ticklish, a sense of being wound up and up all mixed together seeping through my joints and right to the tip of that you-know-what. Because of the strange rocking up and down and back and forth, that game ended very shortly.

"I want to pee," my mouth whispered.

Couldn't. Couldn't break loose. Foot or calf, hooked and held. The increasingly synchronized pressure answering and answering back brought that stiff thing down to the depth of the tingling impalement. Embraces tightened and something shot out with a surprising shudder.

Embarrassing. The briefness was embarrassing. Couldn't stand up, drooped, fell down all soft. The woman nipped, laughing softly. A gift or a plundering? Love or animal instincts? All this melded in phantasmal images that have blazed up on days that torment. Strange! A strange experience!

A strange treat. A young widow, a lump of meat, or a conscience? Or the residue of corroded custom and tradition, now fragile and ragged? It was all so sudden, so passionate, and rather a burning nuisance.

The day passed and I felt grown up.

6

I was close to Tuan Smith. I learned a lot and received a lot of new things from that foreigner. About his origins, his family, where he lived, his education and what was going on in the world. About religion and belief, study, ideals, goals, and the purpose of life. The three of those foreigners quickly mastered the local language.

The ceremony was agreed to. The hornbill. Tonoy, the god of the earth, would be summoned in the form of a hornbill, two days before Tuan Smith and his friends would return to America. The *bulé* were keen to see one of the gods in an actual manifestation. Among the Benuaq people, these are very often represented by animal totems. Spirits that manifest themselves in the flesh and are visible to the eye.

God? Other than symbol? No one has ever been given the opportunity or the ability to see God's true form. God exists, but is in disguise. Like wind, like cloud, like fire, like water. Even like the silence that creeps along the wall, sweeps across the open space in front of the longhouse, ascends the hills, descends into the valleys, caresses the brow and the lineaments of a beautiful face. In all places. In the dry fields, in the lakes, in the forest, in the living spaces of the longhouse, in bed, with one's own lover, in one's heart. So close, yet beyond grasp. God is, but as barely visible as the flickering of a star. At the distance that is the most intimate, in your very heart.

The longhouse was packed to overflowing with residents. Waiting for something extraordinary. A performance that amazed. A savior? Foreigners believe in the crucified one, and here? Rather complicated. So many, many symbols. So many! Birds, objects, spirits, trees and rivers, stones and high mountains. And Tonoy, the god of the earth? Rangkong the Hornbill? Letala Senieng Jatu, the god who brought humankind down from heaven? The Most High?

Uncle Jomoq. He was the one. His were the skills that we relied on. As was the custom, he read mantras, scattered yellow rice grains on all sides, from the west to the east, from the south to the north, sowing and sowing all around where he stood. He stamped, gazed into the sky, stamped three times, his mouth completed the rest of the mantra, mumbling and muttering. Funny as all get out. His spit reddened the sides of his lips. Spit from chewing betelnut and sirih leaf. A filthy sight, rather unpleasant to watch. The foreigners gaped as if possessed, so unique were the healer's mantras in the ceremony.

"She comes from where the sun rises. Drifting with the winds like the *garuda* eagle. Her wings beat in time as she glides so sweetly. The pretty female hornbill, so beautiful," said Uncle Jomoq.

All present were more silent than silence itself.

"She'll stop in a moment on a branch of that *benuang*," he explained, pointing to the tall tree with the cork-like wood, "then swoop down to the middle of the field before us. She will beat her wings again, and perch on that coconut frond as she sings the song of heaven. Her voice is gentle, not like those hoarse and rough-sounding male hornbills. After making a few displays, she'll veer far off and finally disappear where the sun goes down."

The atmosphere was serene, the silence deep. All those present remained mute, not speaking. Everyone waited deep in thought and hope. In confusion and turmoil. Shaking deep inside, hope and disappointment raging. Along with the foreigners, even Uncle

Jomoq's chest shivered. Embarrassing, if the earth flower girl, the first woman to be created, Ape Bungen Tana, did not appear. His breath quavered, his mouth muttered, he repeated mantras. Only the wind kept whistling around them.

"She's coming." Uncle Jomoq opened his eyes and pointed to the east. True. A dot soared in the distance, growing bigger and bigger. Approaching. Finally, the lovely hornbill appeared in clear view. Her feathers and beak were gorgeous, elegant. Her wings opening and closing, opening and closing! She flapped her wings and soared, chuffing and hissing. Everything was just as brief as it had been originally described.

Her playful displays were no less than expected. Complete. But, surprisingly, when she should have soared off to the west, she plunged back down to the arena. Strange! A cobra appeared in the middle of the field. Suddenly the snake struck at the hornbill. Startled, the bird swerved and flapped away. Hastily, wildly— frightened. Her haphazard course took her past the onlookers, her talons scoring Tuan Smith's temple. Several slashes cut his white skin. The spectators ran here and there in confusion and panic.

"Pardon," said Uncle Jomoq, "maybe there was a mistake beyond my knowing. Usually it's always all right and goes smoothly." The foreigners kept nodding. Full of regrets, laughing to themselves. Or muttering disdain. Who knows? In a couple of days, they'd be going back to America. Many memories would be left behind with the residents of the longhouse, and with me too.

For all my life!

7

"It's clear to us, right?" Uncle Jomoq was concluding his explanation. "We have to perform this healing balian, with seeking the imprisoned soul as the main ritual, since this calamity was entirely caused by my being too hasty in my summons and without making any offerings at all. The manifestation we saw wasn't just some kind of show. We were wrong in doing that."

Here I was left all by myself. I heard the council members agree. All costs would be borne jointly. Every *bilik* in the longhouse would contribute according the measure of its ability.

Unconsciously, I drew a long breath. My heart clotted with doubt. Was all that true? Or was it that my own thoughts had gone astray? Thoughts unable to study and analyze the depths of the ancestors' philosophy about truth and salvation? About the meaning of living together and belief?

This sort of adat had of course petrified. It had become our flesh and blood, hard to break free of. Reforms and renewals are not easy, especially if they're not introduced in sympathetic circumstances. No one wants to support change. No one dares to risk bad luck.

Maybe malaria had gotten me. The swamps and marshes are the home of vast clouds of mosquitoes. The stifling longhouse, the dim spaces and rooms, the mess of garbage strewn everywhere. With many people living together, proper care of your health isn't feasible. Lots of people spit, relieve themselves and throw out all kinds of filth wherever they please in places they shouldn't. Flies swarm everywhere. It is mucky beneath the longhouse because of the deposits of sewage and the sluicing of pigs. A riot of smells.

I swallowed a few of the tablets that Tuan Smith had given to me. Gradually my fever receded.

My eyes weren't stinging too much!

8

My favorite souvenir from Tuan Smith was a transistor radio. It seemed nothing in this world was as valuable as that radio. Even though its sound rose and fell, crackled and got very faint, the

songs it picked up every night were really great. Every now and
then, of course, it boomed and hurt my ears, but if new batteries
were put in, the booming wasn't as bad. The singing came through
clear, sermons, speeches, the dialogue in plays and the programs
of various broadcasting stations came through perfectly. He was
a very good guy, that Tuan Smith. The radio often picked up the
language of the *bulé*, but it didn't sound nice to my ears. I couldn't
understand a thing they were saying!

The festive atmosphere of the balian was by now going strong.
It was now the fourth of the eight days planned for it. Visitors
flooded the area. The longhouse was packed, with crowds of people
showing up, especially at night.

There are two sorts of religious ceremonies in this region. They
are considered even or odd. Ceremonies brought about by sadness,
like death, had to be counted as odd. But ceremonies unconnected
with death, as even. Four, eight, sixteen. Counted in geometric
progression.

The sounds of the bracelet and anklet bells clashed with different
musical rhythms. Soft and harmonious. Their rhythm rose and fell
in line with the requirements and atmosphere of the ceremony.

The ceremony's agenda portrayed the healer's search for the
soul. The soul of the sick one was considered missing, a captive of
the angry Tonoy. The palm of his hand now a mirror, the balian
aimed it here and there. A candle of beeswax brightened his way,
wax spread on a rag the size of a little finger. Lit up and placed on
a bowl of raw rice grains. A porcelain bowl filled with votive rice
grains. Placed on the crown of his head and concealed by a black
head scarf. In his hand were leaves of the *kepuding* plant. Red, like
a weapon. He poured his all into the movements, his story relating
a long and dangerous journey. Apprentice healers followed as
attendants. A number of people accompanied him from behind.

This particular ritual was called *balian bawo*. Its ceremony must be done at night with special objects and materials. A headscarf is tied and a necklace hangs around the neck, one of ancient wood and the tusks and fangs of animals considered to possess supernatural powers. *Sumang sawit*, it's called. A metal bracelet, a *getang*, is worn on both wrists. Jingles and clinks when moving. His back is covered with primitive patterns, drawings made with rice flour and limestone. A mid-length skirt called *sempet* covers the lower part of his body and a sash called *sempilit*, with ends dangling alongside each leg, is tied around his waist, and has motifs that portray a world of magic. Shows the healer's heroism and courage. The patterns selected are striking with colorful and festive lacy painting.

The candle kept on glowing on top of his head. The search was pursued. A dance with movements matching the course of an arduous journey that cut across a deep valley. Many dangers were encountered. However, the hiding place of the missing soul remained unknown.

The healers arrived at a resting place to recover from their exhaustion. Even the music stopped, leaving only the chanting of the last of the mantras, immediately answered by the women singers. The ceremony was a conversation in trivialities. The singers asked what difficulties the healers had encountered in their quest. The oldest of the healers told them. They talked back and forth, on and on, for quite a long time!

Another part awaited. It didn't stop until the missing soul was found. When this part of the ceremony was completed, the balian bawo continued on. And would not finish before morning!

Ordinarily, the longhouse people didn't sleep when ceremonies like this were performed. The young men took turns playing its music and the girls took turns in serving the needs of the ritual. They changed the offerings, incense, ceremonial gear and the performances. All sorts of performances, one after another.

Very pleasant moments!

Now was the time. The boys and girls were free to joke and trade teasing insinuations as they take soundings of each other's hearts. Being intimate, even binding themselves with promises to see each other seriously and be in love. These were moments of amusement and distraction, nights that were filled with passion, the arrival of many visitors, young men and women. Meeting, sometimes flirting with their eyes, smiling or turning away in shyness or disdain, keeping quiet, their hands busy with the offerings, striking the musical instruments—it's all play! This was the moment to attack with sweet talk, especially for one that was very pleasing—you can't give up! Not until you've been accepted or rejected.

Nights filled with passion!

Doctors? The healers and their ceremonies are the doctors. There are no doctors here, not in these remote districts. The balian's role is critical in medical treatment and religious ceremonies. Even I can't reject that! Even though I don't believe in this, in my case, the facts spoke for themselves! I began to recover, which really made no sense at all. Even Tuan Smith, the professor, scratched his head. Rubbed his eyes in disbelief. A patient, a girl with a boil on her back. The boil had swollen with pus, very large! And a balian, a healer, still young, male. With a ceremony, cut it open, got rid of the rotten pus, and she was cured. Cured in an instant! No scar, nothing. Not the slightest scar of a wound. A miracle, of course. It made no sense. But that Westerner, Tuan Smith, witnessed it.

The people of this region hold fast to adat, their traditions and customary law. It's hard to penetrate, and that includes the healing ceremony and its healers. This ceremony is just like the work done by health officers. But in a very special way, in a subtly difficult way, in the methods of administering medicine and therapy that must be through the ceremonies, the healer stands alone in his ancient and animist specialty. Not only because his therapy is not based on scientific calculations, but more so because of the special characteristics of its adherents, who are still secluded, isolated. A journey of life in an independence that binds. Because it has become a requirement that the gods demand sacrifices and offerings as a sign of devotion.

It becomes an ongoing cycle whose rotation is fixed. Fixed for all time. In our thousands we go and don't return, and in our thousands we came and welcomed the ancient dawn, in their thousands our footprints disappeared, without a sign, without carved monuments, without memorial columns into which our names have been cut. Like a single leaf. Knocked about by hardship, baked by the sun, cleansed by the rain, shaken by the hurricane. Occasionally, stiffened by cold weather. Then: old, molting, transient. Rot becomes humus, and leaves no trace. There's no bargaining. Not ever.

The ceremony on the longhouse veranda reached fever pitch. Tracked the edge of night. Night climbed toward morning. The cold crept in through the cracks and gaps in the wall. The longhouse was filled with clamor. I shut my eyes to go to sleep, to sleep! At that point, Waning waylaid me. I opened my heavy, drowsy eyes. Waning smiled so very sweetly. The softness and gentleness of an adolescent girl, smiling at me. Caressing and stroking, pleasant-sounding words, a cheerful face. I shut my eyes tight. Waning, I don't want to be troubled by that shadow again. The music outside grew louder, more and more arousing.

"Will you be coming back soon, *Kakak*?" Her head was bowed, in her hand a *linga*, a tool for weeding the dry paddy lands. Her father's fields were broad, and the paddy bowed in waves when pounced on by the wind. Fertile greenness, the stalks upright in their healthy youth. Green as far as the eyes could see. Like life!

"Yeah. After I get all the resin and rattan, bees' wax and honey gathered together, it'll be about enough to cover the ceremony."

"Oh, that's good! But it tortures Waning to wait so long for Kakak."

"It's the same for me too." My words flew out all on their own. "You and I'll work all day long, full of hope for our future. Finally, we'll be together again." Birds swooped over the little grain barns and bathed in the clouds as the wind gently caressed our faces. There was a clear and pure peace in the roaring of our two chests. The sun swiftly shifted into evening.

"All day long I'll work in the fields. At night I'll weave the finest cloth. The moment you come home, brother, the cloth will be finished and ready."

Her eyes were sparkling. The sincerity of her look charmed me into the depths of peace.

"My mother and your mother have agreed to weave our wedding clothes." Her words were joyous and sure. "I'll wear the *ulap* with lace, together with all the little glitters. The full gown and the beaded head band. Mother's prepared the adornments. My hair will hang down freely below my shoulders. You used to praise it for being so naturally black."

I nodded and smiled, and she smiled.

"And of course you'll wear a fringed and tasseled loincloth, the *baju sonang* and the purple head cloth? How beautifully we'll enter the happy days of flowers."

Her words were simple, candid and straightforward. We gazed at each other for a moment. Her countenance was cheerful, a little secretive. Innocent, graceful looking, a face that was soft and gentle. Her heart? Was this a heart that didn't like to share love?

"If, let's say, I don't come back?" I asked, sounding her out.

"Ning will wait. Wait. Wait. Wait! Until Kakak comes back." Her expression turned gloomy, her eyes lost their luster. "Because Kakak will surely return!" Waning said with certainty.

"And what if Ning breaks her promise?"

She looked startled. Her face darkened, her eyes shot arrows into my heart, sliced my heart. Regret beat within me, so crudely had I doubted her faithfulness.

"Waning has chosen Kakak. Kakak alone! Nothing can separate us. Except death. Or if it's Kakak who doesn't keep his promise?"

"I'll be faithful. But I must earn my livelihood. When we separate, for a long time, there's no telling what may happen. Like Sili who left Itung. They say he's happy at Kampung Gunung. But Itung went crazy and plunged into the river."

"It's only a matter of being sure and being faithful. Love is always filled with sacrifice," she said tremulously. Her eyes moistened. Several drops of clear water flowed from them. "I have promised. I will keep my vow of faithfulness and a good conscience. Or does Kakak still doubt me?"

I took her hand. I stroked her loosely hanging hair. Her eyes were still wet. There were sobs from down deep within her breast.

"Tears are no good for a sweet and lovely goddess." I wiped the pools of tears in her eyes. "Now's the time for laughing and love."

Our youth blossomed on waves of hot yearning. I nipped at her pale lips. We tore and tugged at each other greedily and long. Long! Loving hands joined and entwined. And mortal hands do not want to stay still, they creep stealthily in search of all softness. Two pliant little hills making my blood hiss. And now we reached the heat that burns.

There was no watch hut in the fields, no huma crop lands, no birds, no sky, no earth! No growing rice, no wind. There was no day. There wasn't! There was only song. Our song of love. There was only the sun. The sun of our love. Only our love. There was only fire. The fire of our love. There was only the heavens. The heavens of our love. There was only the earth. The earth of our love. There was only breath. The breath of our love. The trees sang sweetly. Sang of our love. The clouds sang. Sang of our love. And the wind plucked at lutes. The lutes of our love. All of nature was singing the tune of love. Our love. Our souls sang. Sang of our love. A beautiful jingle-jangle swaying. That stabbed deeply. That tormented hearts.

It was a long time before we came to. We found ourselves, the two of us, on the top of a field watch hut. Oh, God! The sky was still as it had been. The leafiness, too, just as before. Waving cheerfully. The grasses nodding *salam*. There was an intimate strangeness when our eyes met. She smiled and I smiled.

Like the sky smiling at the earth.

9

At that time, I was sixteen years old and Waning, fifteen. Her mother was a cousin of my mother's, but her father came from a kampung in the districts to the south of us. Her father had been appointed headman to replace my father. My father had replaced my departed grandpa and then been appointed adat head.

Ever since we were small, we were paired off like fighting cocks. But we ourselves saw nothing to object to in this. Everything just went along in the ordinary togetherness of innocent children who didn't know a thing about anything.

After we reached adolescence, our hearts were softly and gently entwined in a curious sort of intimacy. We gazed at each other, laughed or smiled together, on the huma, on the riverbank; wherever we went, we wanted always to be together. If one were without the other, the world was lonely. If one couldn't find the other, it would be unbearable for both, unable to stand the pain. So that our parents' intentions did not meet with any difficulty, nor did ours.

That ceremony, oh yes, that ceremony! Very boring and oh-so tedious. Exhortations and admonishments, sermons, advice, and, yeah, what I couldn't forget, roasted chicken, roasted pig, and forty types of side dishes. Meeting ceremonies, blessing ceremonies, waiting ceremonies. Waiting until I had reached eighteen and Waning seventeen.

We were now engaged.

10

Now, I felt I had truly recovered. I still felt bits and pieces of it all: fatigue, weakness and lethargy, and maybe also aching joints, teeth-grinding pain, and shakiness when I stood up.

Shaky, and with spots before my eyes. Lots and lots of them, and for a long time.

Just a littler earlier today, visitors came in droves to witness the balian. The final night, a lively and happy climax. The ceremony concentrated on rescuing the soul whose place of confinement had been discovered. The soul must be seized, reckless determination was needed, and also very special tools, vehicles, and weapons.

This couldn't fail. Could not! The red dragon with an army of subtle creatures struck the sampan, which almost sank. The oars survived, the helm was nearly broken and Uncle Tunding was dunked into the water. The soul was snatched back from the healers, and they returned in disappointing defeat.

The army of subtle beings was mighty. Tonoy. The god of the earth, the soul-keeper. The fussing old crab, with all his terms and conditions for releasing the soul. Flowers, dedications and offerings, and ceremonies. This! This! And that! Do it according to the terms, according to adat.

Now a different device was selected for use. A *tujang*, symbol of a sampan-shaped flying ship. Again, the balian's assistants were selected. Experienced ones, a bit on the old side, possessing many stratagems and superior wit. Nimble and trustworthy, with many other types of sciences. Because, in addition to confronting a soul-snatching, other balian had different skills and gurus from far-off lands, and they often pitted their skills against each other. They harassed each other, testing out their science—even, and this often happened, killing their opponents by dark means. By the dark sciences, the sciences of the balian!

The concordant thundering of the musical instruments made a non-stop racket. The balian stepped into the tujang, swayed it back and forth. The propellers, the wings, the tail, the control devices, and the destination? It was definite, all of it! One direction, one destination—the soul of the sick one had to be rescued!

The singers sent them off with a *lele*, that is, a sung call for release consisting of only one note and one word. A call and an answer, again and again, over and over. Women, girls, all sang the *lele*. The men stood at the alert, watchful, on guard. Who was guarded against or watched for, was not apparent, ordinary people not being able to guess where it was. *What* it was could not be faced directly like this. Ordinary eyes were earthly eyes. They couldn't see.

The boisterous din of the longhouse, the music and the chanting of the balian, the clinking of the bracelets, the veranda filled with onlookers. The flames of resin and other tree sap flickered and glimmered, glimmered and flickered. People between darkness and light, darkness and light, with all eyes directed at the tujang. One minute, two minutes, several minutes, an hour. Yes, an hour since the tujang had left, getting closer, getting closer to where the soul was imprisoned. The music got louder, the healers became increasingly intense, and the hearts of the spectators throbbed:

Tonoy together with a whole army of red dragons? The healers? Could they snatch back the captive soul?

Mythology? And Tonoy? According to the beliefs of this ethnic group, Tonoy's place, where the soul was imprisoned, was located in a land further into the forest. That god of the earth kept the soul in a seven-cladded copper strongbox! The key had to be fought over. Taken, stolen, or seized. Well, the healers' job was a tough one: seizing a key, opening the strongbox and grabbing the imprisoned soul, and bringing it back. Returning it to its physical host so he might have a healthy life. A healthy life!

This was the place. The betel tree blossoms were hung in front of the tujang, tilted with the *tinting*. Tinting is sticky rice, red sticky rice! All of these are symbols, Tonoy's palace, the key, the copper strongbox, and the tools and accessories of the balian. Images, substitutes, the place, and the snatched rescue. The blossoms were twisted around and around, the tujang was rocked and swayed. Swords, machetes, daggers, and spears were made of *tinting*, with *kepuding* leaf and yellow rice. There were bullets, *kris*, and all kinds of battle weapons. Truly, this was arming for war, and the music! Louder, ever louder! Never stopping, just going on and on, until the longhouse was in a total uproar of noise.

11

Seven of us went on *berahan*, gathering jungle produce. Uncle Lengur was the oldest among us. The five others were over twenty, and I myself was the youngest. Duon and I were not leaving wives and children in the longhouse, because of course neither of us had ever mounted the marriage thrones.

The custom in this region is that when the season for planting rice had passed, the men will leave for the forest in search of resin and rattan, to collect birds nests, beeswax, and honey, to capture pythons and the spotted water snakes, to get bear's bile and crocodile skins, and make the pig and deer jerky that the Chinese like so much.

We would be gone for a long time, months on end. It would almost be harvest time when we returned. It had become part of adat that the wives and children stayed in the longhouse, took care of themselves, fished, went into the fields, even hunted in the forest around the huma clearings. The husbands had no reason to feel anxious, for the togetherness of the longhouse meant their families would never be abandoned or neglected. What lay hidden, beyond this togetherness, were only issues and problems that were deeply personal. Property, marriage, and customs and traditions.

Adat keeps an eye on everything!

This was my first *berahan*. A test prescribed by adat for a young man who very soon would be commencing the new life of marriage. A maturation of both body and spirit, to prepare by oneself all the needs, apparatus, and costs of the wedding ceremony.

Meaningless words? Yes, just about. Because in the end all the required costs would be covered jointly by the longhouse community. That's what adat demands, that's how great the feelings are of *gotong royong*, that is, everyone bearing a burden together, of personal loyalties and pride, especially if the marriage partners come from different *kampung*. The ceremonies must be at their grandest.

But adat can be a two-edged sword. The young man would normally be very reluctant to return home from the forest empty-handed, his shoulders bent low under this spiritual weight. Responsibility, fate, and good fortune affect one's spiritual energy and confidence in the face of the dreariness and the cheer of the days ahead.

The place we selected for *berahan* was considered promising. But it was very far off. Sometimes we stopped paddling in the middle of the night if the weather turned bad or if we had problems at the rapids. The seven of us paddled and slept by turns. Because we had to be alert and at the ready: tigers, bears, crocodiles, or poisonous snakes could suddenly attack our sampan, which often hugged the riverbank.

We stopped on the sixteenth day. Made a hut and prepared what we needed for the days of *herahan*. On the following day we were ready to roam the surrounding forest. Luckily, those woods held much resin, rattan, and *tanyut* trees that were filled with honeycomb hives. The hives dangled from high branches and the wild game was quite unafraid, never having been disturbed before. Just like in the legends? A comforting folk tale? Not at all! It really was that way. Nature around here was virgin, not yet despoiled by human hands.

For three months we gathered up the fruits and produce of the forest. Rafts were prepared and loaded. The water was too shallow, they wouldn't budge. The current couldn't take us. We waited for rain.

In the middle of the fourth month, rain came and the rafts were carried downstream. Our hearts cheered, because we would very soon meet our families with the results of our labors, the fruits of the forest. The riches granted by Letala, our God.

"Your raft is really loaded. Waning will be thrilled to greet you. Just pull you into her embrace." This was Duon kidding.

"But during the nights, hey!" teased Kunta, "Don't be too obvious. Her dad's one of the southern folk, and often gets really het up." Kunta was getting worse and worse. I only smiled, remembering his wife, Kunti. Previously, he had been eaten with jealousy.

"He's been blessed, hasn't he?" said Uncle Langur.

"It doesn't matter, just so long as they don't carry on at the end of his mother's nose."

"How about at the end of the earth?" said Kola.

"At the end of time, which is fast coming," Uncle Lengur chimed in again.

"Yeah, because we'll be getting in tomorrow for sure, right? So no need to hurry. Waning will definitely be waiting." Kunta always wanted to have the last word. His workmates never let a chance go by for jibes and clowning around, a consolation on exhausting days. Humor and stories. Tales or legends. Even dirty jokes that got you all hot and bothered!

We were now on day nine of our downstream trip. If nothing amiss occurred, the rafts would be moored on the other bank tomorrow morning, right opposite the longhouse pier. After a few days' rest, the current would carry our rafts farther on down to the sub-district town. Sixteen days to go downstream!

The pounding in my chest grew stronger and stronger. The farther downstream we got, the more plans I created and brought to bloom. Strong yearnings indeed had piled up from being separated from Waning these past four months. The meaning of lover, the meaning of love, blossomed in a deeper significance than anything I had ever known in everyday life. The pain of being burned is unknown to a person whom fire has not ignited.

Waning, a girl whom I knew right down to the hidden folds of her heart, down to her gentle depths. In her smile, in the stress of her voice and the accents of her speech, the steps she took, the purity of her humanity. Here was a mystical attraction between two bodies, two persons, two souls. Angry... sometimes: a little pinch, avoid speaking and meeting—each tormenting the other. A great intimacy blossomed. Blossomed and flourished in great abundance in two gardens.

That was her, Waning. Angel with the cute wings. Snared me. Snared me with love. With tender love and faithfulness. So in this sense, I felt so tormented.

"Your raft will be tied up over there across from here," Waning had said then. "Stand on top of what you've gotten, Kakak. Waning will be welcoming you there in her own sampan. You will go off again, and then come back to me. Waning is very happy." Her voice both sad and clingy. "Then we will be together. Just we two."

"What if the price of resin and rattan falls and I only obtain a few goods? Would you be disappointed?"

"Brother went out searching. We must be grateful for the good fortune and opportunities that God showers upon us."

"If your parents demand much?"

"Haven't they given us their blessings? Everybody was equally responsible for everything. My parents are your parents too. The amount is not a problem."

"Only for show?"

"You and I are what are important. Us! Only us."

Waning stayed awake almost the whole night through, helping her mother prepare the provisions, various kinds of dry food for the journey. Very busy!

In the cold air of the morning we had the chance for some passionate embracing. Dew bathed the floor of the pier, vapor arose in the air, whitely, silently. None of the fishermen had yet come to the river. We hurriedly fumbled with each other in a throbbing intimacy. The mood of separation pounded our hearts so reluctant to be parted. Love was indeed sweet in the heart and like sugar on the lips.

Yeah, like on a foggy morning, you just can't predict the far-off future. When the world is in fog everyone's visible, you just can't see them clearly. Just keep on supposing the struggle will continue and the wrestling will never end. Oh, damn! Waning's water gourd fell into the river. I dove in.

Waning's mother suddenly appeared at the pier.

"What? Early morning acrobatics? Practicing?" My future mother-in-law had just about caught us.

"Waning's water gourd fell." I was swimming after it.

Her mother glanced over at Waning. The young girl was mortified.

I left later in the morning, no time for just the two of us to be together.

Four months apart, a sharp anguish for a pair of lovers who fused in love. Ripping and shredding!

12

Uncle Tunding had brilliantly and safely seized the key of the copper trunk and brought the patient's soul back home. Each visitor now breathed easy because the patient who had been treated with the balian had been saved.

The music, no longer so earsplitting, now played in a rhythm gentle, refined and calm. The *balian's* story returned to earth and had now came to the ceremony of returning the soul to its owner.

The healers came to me, intentionally laid at a little distance and surrounded by the people who waited, my mother and several girls. Their movements kept graceful time with the music. Their sarongs fluttered and flapped and the rather peculiar smell of incense pervaded everywhere. Smoke assailed my eyes, which I quickly shut. The balian continued the ceremony.

Our seven rafts were moored somewhat upriver from the mooring at the pier. It was busy on the riverbank, lots of people moving all around, back and forth, a bustling crowd! But I didn't see Waning. My pretty dove. Nowhere to be seen among the village people.

This is what happened. Our love story, heartfelt and true. That arose from the warmth of the youthful souls of our entire beings.

Love that discovered the earth, fertile soil planted with belief, struggle, and self-respect. Blood and the life spirit.

This is what happened. Misery hung like a necklace, striking, striking every chest, draining tears, twisting and turning, overwhelming. Grim sorrow stirred up the longhouse, twisting, stamping and kicking. Chaos and noise, and our raft was safely tied, secure! The longhouse shivered.

"Waning's been taken by Jewata! The water god!" Mother rushed over to meet me. Tears bathed her face. "Waning…"

"Jewata?" Reflexively I stared at her. Puzzled! "No! No! No one can take Waning! No one!" I shrieked.

"But she's gone," Mother explained.

"Bear up and be brave, child." Waning's mother embraced me, sobbing. "Waning is still yours, though she's left us. We never could have reckoned on this disaster," she said sobbing. Her tears flowing all down her face.

People swarmed everywhere, the atmosphere deranged. Weeping and wailing fused. A completely unexpected loss. The flower of the village had been snapped off, broken so unnaturally. No trace, no sign. The search looked hopeless. Exhausting, in vain.

I had no strength to shed tears. A wound so profound, the gash of a two-edged sword. I sank into a dark well. Everything black. Black! Black! Oh God! Happiness passed just like that, so fast. A sweet play ending in such grief!

It was only two days later that an old shaman was able to summon the guilty crocodile. At first it was unwilling to respond to the shaman's summons. Too impatient to wait by the riverside, the shaman dove into the water, taking with him a strand of hair of the dead one, and the old crocodile was dragged out with the strand of hair. Dragged right onto the land. Did not argue back. Its tears flowed. My father and Waning's father cut open its stomach.

Waning the cheerful and bright was no more. My Waning, filled with warmth, elegant, capable, and intelligent. No young radiance, blooming and fecund. Nature, so cruel and fierce. Snatched away life and love. Smashed happiness just then budding.

My Waning, what curse is this? You had to bear the suffering, to bear this error and apostasy! Horrifying, a body not whole, cut up into pieces, the prey of a hungry old crocodile.

Each piece of the body was removed with care, one by one. Put together in human form that was intact.

Waning's mother and my mother, several women who were family members, could bear it no more. Exploded in weeping that grew ever more uncontrolled. An event that shook our quiet village to its roots with its burning, slashing pain.

Later, the burial day of Waning. The burial of my love. My ill-starred lover. With my own hand I carved her an exquisite coffin. I had given her no devotion other than the heat of my youth, other than my hopes and ideals. What I had harvested with the sweat of my body was nothing at all.

Her weaving truly had been completed. Beautiful, so beautiful. There was embroidery that pictured our holy love. Our bridal clothes. Only the inner parts still awaited final refinement. But now it was all pieces in disarray. It couldn't be otherwise. Just let Waning take everything with her. I did not want those things becoming the burden of a memory that would only drag on and on.

Waning had gone home to the Deity and could never come back.

Everywhere was in twilight!

13

Very early in the morning all the parts of the *balian* ceremony were finished. Signs for *jariq*, the ritual prohibition against visiting to socialize upon the completion of a balian, were put up all around the longhouse. These were notices for outsiders to respect the period of prohibition. People who had not visited during the days of the balian were not permitted to come up into the longhouse. Heavy claims would be levied against violators, particularly if the subject of the *balian* ceremony relapsed or died. According to adat, all costs would be borne by the violator.

One by one, the guests returned to their homes. The longhouse was quiet again. I was able to rest with greater calm. I slept, ate meals, strolled about, slept again, sat around and exercised my stiff and achy muscles. From time to time, I sweated in the steam concocted from various kinds of boiled tree leaves. I was wrapped up and steamed from below. Until the sweat came out and layers of grime peeled off, and my body looked all wrinkled and skinny.

Moments of anxiety. Days of boredom. Making my memories of Waning all the more punishing. The bracelet I had given her was still around her wrist. Her ring, still whole, on her finger. But that arm was not whole. It was off from her shoulder. Its fingers swollen up. The body all torn up, some parts still missing. Missing! Eaten by other animals or fallen to the ground who knew where. Truly, truly painful to think about!

On her water gourd were little scratches, a hundred and fourteen of them. A hundred and fourteen days I was gone after Waning took water with her gourd. On the one hundred and fourteenth day, the hungry crocodile devoured her. On the one hundred and fifteenth day, I came. But Waning had gone on the morning of the previous day. Yes, just yesterday morning!

I still felt warmth in my chest.

III

Kewangkey: Burying the Bones

Verses often sound from the mouths of the longhouse people, in work chants, whistling, or songs glorifying our village, often sound from the mouths of the longhouse people. People here are always full of songs. Their spirits are high and lively. Simple good cheer is often chanted and resounds in every corner of the village.

> *Trees whose leaves give shade*
> *There all find a shelter made,*
> *Our love so now heartfelt*
> *Holy affection in caresses spelt...*

Rinding, meaning shady trees—that's the name of our village. It's a small place, very isolated. Stuck into an upcountry riverbank.

The longhouse stands on a piece of somewhat elevated flatland, surrounded by various kinds of fruit trees and high-soaring coconut palms. Seen from downriver or from upstream it is clearly visible, because the longhouse stands right above a straight river front.

Rather far downstream, the river forms a bend. Because of the frequent landslides and land shifts, this bend is growing wider. Its east side juts out in a promontory. To the west, the hollow of the bend forms a deep cove, Bundon Cove they call it. Most of the people of our kampung consider it haunted. That is because in *ngayau* times a fierce battle took place here. Many perished on both sides. Nonetheless, the attackers were finally crushed. The dead of the defeated force sprawled all over the place.

That happened long ago, but during the dark of the moon, you often hear shouts and cheers and laments and weeping in that inlet. Our elders say that these are voices of the spirits of the soldiers who perished in that *ngayau* battle. Their blood shrieks out for life, because they died before their time. Bad luck and calamity sent swords, spears, and sabre-like *mandau* to hack at their bodies and rob them of their breath. Thousands of corpses all along the inlet had to go unburied by the kampung folk. These are the corpses that shriek their grisly cries when the moon is dark.

Some several kilometers upstream from the longhouse, there is a jumping-off spot used by pigs. During the *langui* season when wild pigs cross the river, the kampung people usually head them off at the steep slopes. Herds of them are ambushed as they cross. The forest life that continues to be led by current generations shows the peculiar character of this remote forest community. They suckle and clutch at, eat and warm themselves from nature. From the forest. In that way, nature is generous in its ferocity.

Were we to stand on a place of high ground, the longhouse would look as if shrunk to miniature squeezed in by mountains soaring to the sky like towers. In the west stands Mount Murray, a doughty soldier faithfully protecting the village. In the north thrusts up Mount Merangah. To the southeast, Mount Meratus towers over extended clusters of hills. Like ancient warriors who continue to live on and stand watch for all time. Far to the south stretches a forest that holds natural wealth, to the east the river winds and bends and scores the island with a gaping wound. Every year the river floods. The inhabitants along the river build stilt houses so as not to get into the clutches of the flood, and the fields are divided into two. The *dempak* fields, that is to say, the bottomland reached by the flood waters, and the mountain fields.

Because of the mud caused by the flooding all along the bottomland, the crop yields of the dempak are usually better than those of the mountain fields. But if the floods come during the wrong season, the bottomlands will be swallowed up and destroyed by the raging waters. Furthermore, flooding in this region usually lasts for more than a month, so that the crops and all the plantings in the dempak will rot in such a prolonged immersion. Thus, kampung people always create fields in reserve.

The results of this year's harvest were quite gladdening. Rain fell often while the huma rice was still young. But the rainfall wasn't excessive and so there were no floods. After the rice burst forth from their swollen stalks, clouds frequently hung in the sky, but the only thing that fell at night was dew. After the rice was plump, the sun provided the right amount of heat to ripen the full-bodied clusters. The villagers were happy because the hillside fields brought good yields. All the crops grew in fruitfulness.

2

In this region, death is a burden for everyone. The deceased can gain prestige and salvation if the conditions of the death ceremony can be successfully met. The bigger and more costly the ceremony performed by the heirs, the greater the benefits in Lumut. So, besides lifelong acts of religious practice, virtue, sincerity, purity, and honesty in this world, the role of the family is also decisive. The departed souls who have not been given the *kewangkey* ceremony will slither and creep about in misery outside the walls of Lumut. Their deeds cannot yet be weighed and balanced so long as kewangkey has not been performed for them. And during this period of waiting, they often disturb the family they have left behind, for such spirits still freely wander the face of the earth.

My grandfather and grandmother died the same year that I had reached ten years of age. The plan for holding kewangkey had long been planned by Father and the village elders, but over the past years, the results of the harvests were disappointing. The years went by and the plan kept getting postponed from one date to the next.

To realize the kewangkey ceremony, the deceased must go through preliminary ceremonies, in accordance with his or her level and prestige. Generally, the corpse is placed in the coffin, a hollowed-out tree trunk known as *lungun* that serves as the receptacle of the remains, and on the seventh day, a kind of half-way burial ceremony is held. The lungun is not buried, but placed in the *garey*, a little hut near the burial plot. A year or two later, the bones are taken from the lungun, and then a second half-way burial ceremony is performed, called *nulang*. The bones are put into an antique earthenware jug, and interred in a burial spot shaped like a cave. This burial place is called a *rinaq*. Usually, valuable belongings of the dead one are also buried in this rinaq.

If the departed was someone who was well-regarded, a *selong* would be used for the lungun, that is to say, a coffin of larger dimensions, one with pictures and painting carved in a way suitable to this person's rank during his or her lifetime. Then, and only after a sufficient amount was paid, the *kewangkey* ceremony was held, the final burial ceremony, whereby the bones of the deceased were set to rest in a *tempelaq*, a hanging coffin, normally of ironwood. The soul of the dead one would be safe and tranquil and find everlasting happiness after the completion of this ceremony. The heirs, too, would feel relief since their debt had been paid. That is because our people are here in this world to serve and be filial. He or she never asked to be here, but it was the nature of that filial honor that cast him or her into this transitory world.

Ordered him or her to be here!

3

The sounds of *domek*, the funeral dirges, billowed and rolled sadly. The spirit mediums had begun the ceremony. Since this is a funeral ceremony, an odd number is the basis of calculation. They decided that this *kewangkey* would be three times seven days. Quite long, three times seven days—three weeks! Yes, those bones... the kampung wished for it that way. Kinfolk of all degrees gathered, a great number of bones were gathered, many families from other villages joined to bury the remains of their own family members, so that the wandering spirits of their homes could be all together. Suspended there, in the tempelaq, in Lumut!

The expenses and the materials? They were kampung people, crying with each other, laughing with each other. Sharing burdens. One would cut down, one would shoulder, with most of the needs managed by themselves. Raw rice, firewood, salt made by boiling the brackish waters deep in the forest. Sugar was tapped from the *enau* palm or pressed from cane. Cooking oil? Coconuts were scraped to make oil, wild pigs hunted during their *langui* river-crossing season. The wild pigs of the forest, how rich in fat they were! Water buffalo, cows, by the dozens! Readied for years on end, for years!

Adat? The hands of adat grip with the talons of demon giants. The hands of belief cage with dogma and maledictions. The *salung*, the outsider guests for the length of the kewangkey ceremony, are the responsibility of the host. Food and drink, the payment to the shaman mediums, ceremonial apparatus and requirements, and all the odds and ends. Holding a kewangkey ritual is expensive!

The southern part of the longhouse veranda became the center of the ceremony. Decorations were appropriate for the purpose and its symbols, equipment and clothing, bowls, and colors. Colors gray and gloomy. Decorations for the ceremony hanging everywhere!

Songs? Only one song may be sung while the kewangkey was underway. The *ngakey* song. Call-and-response singing. Cornering and counter-cornering, attacking and counterattacking, asking and posing riddles. This display of ngakey was lively indeed. The spectators were free to side with whatever ngakey singer they chose to, whichever one they championed.

4

Whenever death occurs, besides letting their tears flow, the people of this region show their sorrow by the women cutting their hair until its fringe reached only down to the shoulders. And even, in the olden days, when the deceased was one's husband, the woman shut her eyes with wood putty or latex for several days, a week, a month, with some able to do so for up to three months. The men, on the other hand, would fast and a undergo *askese*, the repression of lusts and worldly appetites. Periods of mourning: gloomy, sad, and painful.

The first week of kewangkey? The souls are summoned, invited from their dwellings. Invited to the longhouse, to the ceremony arena. Given offerings, various foods, local snacks, sticky rice cakes, bread, all their favorite cooking while they lived on earth. Made as completely and deliciously as possible, and presented on a copper salver, all kinds of food, and so much of it, too! The shamans invited these spirits in to dine, to taste the cooking served by the children and grandchildren.

Living people may not taste these. Such offerings can make one accursed, so only dogs and animals can partake of them.

Animal feast.

The souls are led to wherever they had walked in their lifetimes. To rattan plantations, to other *kampung*, to the rivers, to the towns. They had to repeat every piece of work they had ever done on this earth. Such requirements are what made people here able to walk the straight and narrow path, to be honest and never insincere throughout their lives. So that during their lifetime, they would rarely meet with the bumps and jolts of terrible events.

Sticky rice cooked in bamboo sections, local snacks and edible contributions, cooking. Chickens and pigs are always slaughtered in odd-numbered amounts every day at dusk. This is when the wandering souls have a wild feast and great fun.

Spirit party.

5

During this second week, the people can hold cockfights. All sorts of large-scale games are run. A special hut is set up for the players, and entertainments and performances are provided to the spectators.

During the intervals between the ceremonies are the times for the shamans to dance the *ngerangkau* dance. Another dance permitted is the *tumandang* dance. This dance has a violent quality to it, as it has to be followed by another dance called *mengkopes*, which involves two dancers hitting each other with rattan and warding off the blows with shields. They are turned loose into the middle of the circle like fighting cocks and engage in combat, really fierce stuff. The dancers' bodies get bruised and red, and sometimes the rattan draws blood. Like from the slashing blows of the gladiators!

Music accompanies the tumandang dance. Kettles and drums. The dancers swerve into the center of the circle and contenders one by one present their challenges. Strutting like warriors, they demonstrate their fighting moves. But if the performance gets too violent, the judges will calm them. Will separate the violent dancers!

The third week. Many outside visitors arrived. Came in droves. Came from far-off *kampung*, men, women, and children. The longhouse rooms were packed tight, the ritual structures for the balian, temporary sheds, all were crowded tight. Crowded with visitors.

The program went on and on, the mediums serving the needs of the souls of the dead. Serving them as best they could, for this was their final earthly suffering. The right to enter into the life and freedom in Lumut would be granted to them after the ceremony ended. These spirits would be eternally at peace in their new existence.

I was now nineteen years old. With my natural youth I couldn't survive in a fixed establishment. Many times I discovered village flowers blossoming in their perfection, tickling awareness of my boiling lust. Bah! The images of my lust, the previous experiences with young and pretty widows, strange offerings. That set a man's wishes and desires ablaze.

My parents proposed Ifing as my life's companion, but I still wanted my freedom. Besides, I met Intu from Kampung Ulu. A figure quite to my taste, the naturalness of a perfect young girl who just drove me crazy. With simple make-up, the generous smile on her lips made her look angelic. But our cat-and-mouse love couldn't last long. Even though we groped and fumbled in a tight embrace, mashed our lips together in smoldering kisses, it turned out the girl who ensnared me was already betrothed.

The sacred decapitating knives would have spoken had adat not been sitting there in the middle. Our people are often pigheaded over the smallest stuff. The men more often than not speak wordlessly with the blowpipe and the sword blade. Survive by conviction and the law of the jungle. Self-respect and family honor are often calculated with the price of lives.

I left behind an *antang*, which is an heirloom earthenware jug, in Kampung Ulu. Adat dictated I do so. The language of adat is expressed in antang. Values and norms are defined in antang. The relative worth of a person is the total of his antang. A fine of one antang is what I had to pay for what was considered disturbing a girl who had already been spoken for.

The ritual knives, spears and blowpipes. These were the language of olden times. The souls of men often went flying due to something simple, stupid, or fanatic. Group squabbles, woman issues, property, dwellings, and, most idiotic and uncivilized of all, the feeling that one is a hero if he has hacked off the head of innocent people without any reason. Barbarians! Headhunters!

So! This was the place. The longhouse. The group could peaceably gather here. Collective force could be driven away by collective force. Headhunters, wild animals, snakes, floods, or earthquakes. But fires? Fire is what often turns the communal holdings into ashes. Fire is pitiless. The wood of buildings is great fodder for fire. Garbage, dry leaves, or tough jungle savannah grass feed fires that torch longhouses into ash. Children's hands, children playing, cause fires. From flint stones or dry rice husks.

The longhouse. There it is. A long house, supported on pillars of ironwood. Too high for you to poke at it with a spear. Headhunters couldn't spear anyone on top of the longhouse.

The *ngerangkau* dance pulled me in deeper and deeper, the musical accompaniment together with the funeral songs shifted into a slow rhythm. Mournful and heartrending. This was the moment the women erupted in lament. This was the atmosphere for weeping, weeping in song for the wandering souls. The women lamented together. Mentioned all the goodness of the souls for whom this burial of the bones, this kewangkey, was being performed. The souls of the family, the ancestors, the husband, the wife, or children.

The din of a choir of weeping.

Heartrending!

6

Seven water buffalos would be slaughtered at the end of this ceremony. The hardwood *belontang* statues, to which they'd be tethered, were ready to be carved in seven different ways to commemorate the ceremony. And planted in an open space. Seven open spaces, so the buffalo wouldn't bump into each other when they were let loose to roam about, rattan ropes tied around their necks and to the belontang. Their distance from each other was the length of these ropes.

The carving of the *tempelaq*, the hanging coffin, was finished. It was finely wrought, reliefs that depicted the love and eternal life in Lumut. Several parts showed the living struggle against nature, the origins of this race and its livelihood. In another part were illustrated the foundations of the people's beliefs, pictures of the gods and goddesses, arranged by rank, and the love of two sweethearts, a pure love ended by calamity. But they were united in Lumut, loving each other in a seething intimacy. The hands of the gods helped these two lovebirds.

In another part was Cinta—Love—which depicted the deity Senieng Jatu lowering humanity down from Cinta on Lumut to this world. Being given the knowledge, the desire, the cleverness and skill, to control nature. Equipped with the tools and the means to subdue nature. The better class of people, the advantaged ones who never worked, who were too clever and considered dangerous—these were the ones who were lowered to earth, to sweat and experience the burden of suffering.

Langkar? This was the device that lowered mankind down into this world. Langkar or *pelangkaq,* it was called! Painted on the coffin. Along with the village to which they had been lowered, the number of people who had descended, the tools employed to maintain their lives on earth, the requirement of giving names to their offspring, objects and livestock. The ways and methods of this new life were also depicted in finely-worked carvings. Also the symbols, customs and traditions, laws and marriage, all sorts of ceremonies, permitted dedications and offerings, pets, and all manner of friends in nature. Because the human condition was lower than at its origin, therefore they had to organize praise to the higher "Essence", called Letala.

The ceremony in the longhouse was now over. Now it had moved to a shed-like structure on the ground below. A variety of these had been set up for the worship ceremony. And cockfighting? The cocks were matched against each other, the cocks of Lumut against the earthly ones. Symbols, depictions of the life of the people of the world and the spirits of the dead in the afterlife. The spirit roosters must be defeated for the victory of the dead person's soul. Physically destroyed, but the spirit survives and wins.

The funereal sounds of *domek* resounded along every pathway and lane. The tightly played music rose and fell in the final song of sadness. Since evening, the shaman mediums had performed rituals in the buffalo sheds. This was the heart of it all, the slaughter of the buffalos which symbolize the end of earthly suffering.

The buffalos were decorated. Their bodies were clothed with various ornaments symbolizing the woes of the world. Trident spears, a symbol of endurance, were attached to both horns. On the tails were tied *sompun*, a fragrant kind of swamp tree bark, whose ends now had been burned. Fire symbolizes the life that is filled with warmth on Lumut. Also on the tails were attached bands of rattan. All these decorations were of dull and gloomy colors. Shackles of the physical life of humanity.

The *selampit*? The buffalo tether, connected to two bands of rattan, one around the animal's neck and one around the belontang! Plaited rattan, tetherings for the buffalos to be slaughtered in the ceremony. The buffalo were free to move about in a circle determined by the length of the selampit, round and round all along the slaughtering field. How wretched!

So then! This was the moment that the old spirit medium let loose with a spear into the body of a buffalo. The animal, crazed by the sharp pain, broke down its pen. The spearmen were ready at the edge of the field, spear, sword, dagger in hand, naked! Wherever the buffalo ran and lunged, the selampit held it fast until the people had the chance to stab it.

This is the method of slaughter for the kewangkey ceremony. The suffering animal was a symbol of earthly misery that would soon be left behind. The moment the buffalo pitched forward to the ground and its spirit rose into the air, at that very moment too, the spirit of the dead one was released through this ritual to ascend into Lumut. After the bones had been placed in the *tempelaq*, the gates of Lumut were opened and the spirits were welcomed in with a grand feast in the eternal home.

A feast for the souls of the departed ones!

A special tempelaq had been made for my grandparents. Their skeletons, now clean and drying, were laid out together like a bridal couple sleeping during the nights of their honeymoon. In another part of this coffin were placed the bones of Waning, her body no longer whole, with parts of it missing, not found in the belly of the crocodile that had made her its prey!

On Waning's tempelaq I carved a mark, a memento of our love that had come to nothing. For the last time, I saw again the silent skeletons. Ahhh! My beloved Waning! It was an unfinished story I carved in melancholy shapes. I could compose nothing else. I couldn't properly portray the signs of my faithful love. Or the signs of my deeply felt mourning. All that could be carved was merely symbols of my spiritual composition that knows no end. Grooves with disguised scratchings, secrets that could be understood and enjoyed by me alone. All the memories that draw me into a cycle of events that left me soaked and scorched… who in panic and confusion sinks to the very bottom of the deep. And when I come up, the emptiness yields a vast boundlessness. A stretch of open field where the sun's rays sting without mercy. I see myself there, in silence and in suffering.

The lid of the tempelaq was slowly tightened down. Closer, closer, and finally flush. The top and the bottom edges of the coffin were flush. The two edges were one. Inside Waning lay mute and rigid. Does the soul find salvation in this? Has it flown off silently to live for all eternity on Lumut? I don't know for sure. Not quite convinced. Don't really understand. The beliefs of the people here are too abstruse. Demand too much. Meanwhile, the people as a group simply melt and dissolve. As spoke the ancestors, so speak their descendants. In such a way, adat demands its adherents follow behind in a very long procession, one that is endless! Endless to the very end of time.

When the crowd broke up, from the distance I looked back once more. The tempelaq hung mute and still. Evening fell in growing grayness. *Ahhh, my Waning! Slowly your bones will disappear, ground by time.*

7

"What, daydreaming?" The voice of a girl at my side. I had been sitting by myself on the newly built cleansing *balai-balai*. We call it a *baley tota.*

"About Renta," I said with a laugh. The girl was embarrassed. Her name was Renta. Our hearts were hitched together. All during the days of kewangkey, the two of us often gulped down delicious happiness. Together, in a form of love that was unaffected and simple. Not very balanced. I myself was often indecisive in my stupid lack of understanding.

"Now that's a lie, for sure. You're daydreaming about someone else." She laughed prettily. "Pretty soon, you'll forget all about Renta."

"An episode worth remembering. I'll be remembering her for a long time, for a very long time!"

"Remembering her?"

"Yeah!" I said quickly.

"Who?"

"Renta.'

"No!"

"Yeah!"

"No, no, no, no…!'

"Yes, yes, yes, yes…!"

"No!"

"Renta."

"Not Renta."

"What if it *is* Renta?" I asked.

"What if it *is* Renta?" she asked.

I couldn't answer right away. A girl lively, pretty, affectionate in a motherly way, and elegant. To a certain extent, I liked her. I like softness, I like beauty. Our brief acquaintance brought a different atmosphere into that agitated existence of mine. I, who was often beset by calamity. Who had fallen. Who felt the pain of a wounded spirit. Who, aware of that, was trying to stand up on his own two feet.

"And what if it *is* Renta?" she persisted.

An odd feeling seeped into my chest roiling with doubt. This sweet and pretty girl who appeared before me was a great contrast to Waning and Ifing. Those two actually didn't differ greatly. Could I accept Ifing as a substitute for her older sister who had been lost?

Back then, Waning had never come up with weird thoughts, or suspicious or doubtful words. Maybe because she wanted to drain the cup of this life with me to its last drop. Death was outside and she never gave it a thought. There were the two of us in a warmth that lingered on and on. We didn't want to share. No, we didn't! But now, would Waning be happy to see me falling into the embrace of her younger sister or slumber peacefully, cuddled by this other girl?

Renta stared at me, waiting for me to answer her. But I couldn't. No, I couldn't! There was nothing I could say in reply. I didn't want to play-act, be confused with this episode now, the one before, and shades of the future, in round after round of turbulent mental uncertainty. Turbulence that suddenly turned me into a doubter and all mixed up in the face of persistent pressures and attacks.

Salung? Oh, right, this was the final day for visitors to be guests of the kewangkey ritual. Tomorrow, Renta would go home. Back to Kampung Ujung. So, now was the moment to search for and find firmness. To knot together the final words.

Odd. My mind just went blank. This attack suddenly floored me like someone's old blunt razor. Thank goodness, the bathing ceremony would soon be held, cutting short the time to pressure me. Throngs of people milled around us. Others were filling the ritual baley tota, awaiting their turn to be bathed.

8

The kewangkey ceremony is rooted in sadness. While this is being performed, not a single form of joyous ritual can be carried out. Thus, to start the new day free from weeping and tears, the bathing ceremony, *nota*, has to be held. Everyone who lives in the longhouse must be bathed with water that has been blessed and strewn with flower blossoms. Symbolically, this rite is intended as a cleansing and baptism of people from the ones they were into ones who would undergo a new life. Released from calamity and want, released from sickness and sorrows, released from dangers and hunger, released from envy and prejudice, released from death and now heading for life. Because they had been freed from the influences of the souls of the deceased, whether man or woman, for whom the kewangkey had not yet been performed.

Now the ceremony was over. The debts had been paid. All that was left was the bad luck and good that fate had in store for us. Adolescent boys and girls would try to find a congenial and happy match. The old folk would hope for long life and sustenance and much good fortune. An abundance of happiness and peace all the days of their lives. Mothers and fathers would hope for healthy children, who would grow and flourish in an atmosphere of safety and tranquility. A new generation to manage the fields and groves and perpetuate the generations and customs of the longhouse. Who would hold fast to the adat laws and rituals of the ancestors.

All sorts of flowers were finely sliced and mixed with a watery rice flour batter called *burey*, which was then put into large jars filled with water. The balian masters used this water to wash away grief and sorrow and renew the people of the longhouse.

Musical instruments were played during this ceremony. One by one, the longhouse folk, beginning with the aged ones and ending with the children, were all sprinkled with this water. After this was finished, everyone went into the river, bathed, and replaced their mourning clothes with new apparel that no longer showed the color of grief. A joyful atmosphere was intentionally created as the start of happy days.

As a closing, the thanksgiving rite to the gods called *pesengket nayuq* was held. The longhouse people all enjoyed themselves, cheering and singing their hearts out. There was no more gloom, no more worries and doubts. Grief and debts had been paid, had been redeemed by payments and the sweat and toil of the ceremony.

I followed all the parts of the ritual fed-up and bored. My heart and thoughts were divided between Ifing and Renta. Who in the end could tie down my free spirit and body? Everything was still all confused. Where was the eternal harbor for me to wrap up these wild adventures?

My voice echoed within me. Complete silence, no reply. On top of that, in tears, Renta begged me for a firm answer. The breath in my chest still quivered in doubt. Right up to when, with a final wave of my hand, I sent Renta back to Kampung Ujung, I was still confused.

Confused!

IV

Nalin Taun: The Ceremony of Offering

1

And so, like that, time passed the way pirates do, leaving all sorts of events behind. Grandpa Kuleh went missing, attacked by a crocodile. Not one of the shamans was able to find him. Intong fell from the honey tree when removing a honeycomb. His body was smashed, like Tamir's, torn to pieces by a bear. A cobra killed a girl barely into her adolescence. Her father and mother nearly went mad because she was their only daughter. But, the number of newborns kept shooting up. Several young mothers even gave birth to twins.

The hot dry season lasted rather long this year, but before all the paddy was harvested in the bottomlands, floodwaters came and submerged the greening shoots, turning them into fish chow. At the same time, the yields of the hillside fields were disappointing due to the prolonged heat. The soil became desiccated and the paddy stalks stunted. Even the clusters of rice, which in their youth were healthy and fruitful, wilted and died in the heat. Only bananas, cassava, the various kinds of taro, and the wild yams planted in mountainside fields kept their luxuriance. But the lowland crops were devoured by the floods.

Our village elders were busy with calculations and predictions. For sure, everything that happens has its roots in something. The taboo marriage of Uncle Ningir with Sitoy, who, being his niece, was kin, though not in a straight line. Such a forbidden marriage is called *sumbang*, meaning incest, and was the cause of poor seasons, the unproductive fields, unripe fruit dropping from the trees, difficult hunting, and the occurrence of various kinds of bad luck. Guilt like this had to be redeemed by a ceremony. Uncle Ningir must cleanse the blood of them both until it was the same degree. Hold the ritual of *nalin taun*, slaughtering a white chicken, a white pig, and a white buffalo. Their marriage had to be validated through rites both complex and very costly.

Their kinfolk and the longhouse residents also had to be washed from the stains of that guilt. The land, the ancestors, and the gods included.

What about outsiders? Foreigners? A different hypothesis argued that this calamity was rooted in the arrival of new people who often acted high-handedly. They erected barracks on the riverbank and cut down trees in the forest. Meranti, keruing, bengkirai, ulin, and other kinds of trees were felled. Some of those outsiders even took village women as their wives.

The logs were carried downstream by the current to the mouth of the river. The wives of those foreign men gave birth, but many wives and children were simply abandoned because the men had disappeared to no one knew where. Then new men came, and they did the same. The barracks shifted here and there along the river, the forests were stripped bare, with only new shoots visible, and then abandoned.

"This is a new disaster," Uncle Kosang said. "The peace and quiet of the longhouse has been disturbed by damned scoundrels!"

Uncle Lesan backed him up. "What's painful is that my daughter was left behind just like that, without any provisions. Her husband went downriver on a raft. Went and never came back. She's got twins. So sad. Their mother is so badly off."

"You mean Firama?" Grandpa Mutar broke in loudly.

"Yes, my daughter Inte married that damned Firama! Typical outsider. I was against it from the start. She was asked for by Sudang, you know. But Inte picked that bad-luck Firama!"

"It's possible he's gone back to his own land," offered Uncle Lesan hopelessly.

"Just get her married off if any youngster asks for her," suggested Uncle Kosang.

"Who would want to propose marriage? There are plenty of girls around. But my child is damaged goods," said Uncle Lesan bitterly.

"Marriages like this have become an epidemic. I've heard that it's the same in other *kampung*," Grandpa Piok now said.

"Lots of women and girls south of here got knocked up. The moment the child was born, their husbands went away. And there's been no news of them. To say nothing about providing the means to live," complained Jintok. He had just come back from there. The word was, his own girlfriend had been hooked by a foreigner. He himself had gone nuts. The foreigner had almost gotten a spear run through him. Luckily, his fighting arts were good and the kampung people got things calmed down and let him go. But that guy gave Jintok's girl a big belly.

The longhouse veranda was the arena of heated discussions in the evenings, when the kampung folk usually gathered there after returning from the day's work. The men who had gone pole fishing, net fishing, seine fishing would stop for a moment to hear the latest stories. Especially if one of their fellow residents had just returned from another kampung, since new stories were like a tasty meal in this isolated region.

Traffic and communications here were primitive in the extreme. Their village was a kind of reserve area that would disgust people who were not bound by blood to this land of the longhouse.

The outside world closed itself to the eyes of the people here. Thus, news and stale events out there seemed like hot stuff, to be gossiped about by many mouths in the longhouse.

"I've heard that Renta also got snagged by an outsider," Duon probed. "And I also heard that she went with her husband overseas," he added with more certainty.

"Could be," I replied casually. And, yeah, from the gossip, I had heard that Renta had married a logger, a foreigner! I caught a sense of their relationship when she and I had again met on occasions after that. It's hard for me to trust a girl who's too much of a daredevil.

Over the past few years in this region, there was indeed a plague of marriages between the kampung girls and foreign workers. This situation was hard to avoid, because our own people couldn't match the appeal of foreigners. Especially if these outsiders were handsome and gave lots of presents, the simpleminded girls would be easily seduced. A social phenomenon that spread like the plague here!

On the negative side, such marriages were hard to preserve. That's because the outsiders were here only for a limited period of time. When their contract was over, so was the marriage. The uncomplicated village girls never imagined this. What they hoped for was lasting happiness, since the husband gave them quite a lot of things.

According to adat law, such marriages were valid. But the weakness of adat was that it wasn't written down. The force of evidence couldn't be brought to bear against the foreigners to whom civil law specifically applied. Weak evidence could not work here!

That's why the kampung people were unable to demand compensation or division of the couple's joint property acquired through marriage, for it never occurred to them to get a written agreement about such things, their way of thinking being still quite unspoiled. All that was left were the children without fathers. All that was left were the wives without husbands. The children grew like the wild trees in the forest. Never knew from which tree they had sprung.

In the minds of the kampung people, these events were what caused so many calamities and deaths, such misery, and such bad seasons, because the weather brought only stinking wind and clouds. The rains that came were the rains of disaster. The heat that radiated was a heat that scourged. The people's nighttime songs were no longer as sweet-sounding as they had been in the past. The voices were quavery. Like lamentations. Like tears that stung. The wind brought weeping, the weather brought weeping. Weeping that went on and on. The weeping of the village, the weeping of the forest. The crying of children. The weeping of wives who locked up grief inside themselves.

2

"Nalin taun, there's no other choice," I heard Father say decisively. "A lot of bad things have hit our village, but we've just kept quiet. Don't all those things have to be cleansed so that our village can be cleansed? And us along with it?"

"And those outsiders, too," Uncle Lengur added. "We are guilty before the gods for giving in too much."

"They've also got to bear responsibility!" offered Kojok.

"It's no use our casting blame on others," Father continued. "The important thing is that we re-discover ourselves. That we become ourselves. Not other people. Especially when we're in an atmosphere of crisis, vulnerable even." He was a bit longwinded.

"But what's most troubling and humiliating for us are those foreigners," said Kojok stubbornly. "We're being taken advantage of in big way. The forest and the women."

"What's important in this discussion is, do we agree and are we able to hold a nalin taun or not? We aren't having anything to do with the foreigners!" insisted Father with words that brooked no opposition.

"At least we can ask for support." Kojok was rather deflated from his emotional flare-up.

"No need!" the other elders replied, almost with one voice.

"That'd be shameful! We're no beggars!" yelled Uncle Kedis.

"We are a mighty people. It's always been forbidden to go begging!"

"Didn't Uncle Ningir agree to go half the cost?"

I glanced at Ningir, who was grinning. "Half the funds that we collect together," I suggested.

I saw the elders nod. And so it was decided that the nalin taun ceremony had to be performed as soon as possible, before the kampung went back to their busy work in the fields. Before other troubles occupied the longhouse residents!

3

I felt my introduction to Rie was the most natural of meetings. And actually we really must have been brought together by supernatural hands. There was a compatibility that attracted us to each other from deep inside. So that duality is the happiness that adorns youth throughout the tumultuous desires of its adolescent soul.

At first, we were simply attracted and captivated by each other. There was no plan. Everything happened unexpectedly. I, the admiring fan, and she the dazzling goddess of the stage. In fact, we first got to know each other from something totally trivial.

She was the daughter of the headman of Kampung Bawo. Many visitors came to watch the nalin taun ritual there. At night, Rie was the lead dancer of the gantar dance. And, damn, wouldn't you just know it, the guests were asked to join in the program. I was dragged to the middle of the arena. And as an honor, we outside visitors had to dance with the girls. Rie swayed as their leader and I was appointed to lead the boys. The air was lively with the cheers and shouts of the spectators. But the damned thing was, on the morning of that day as we were watching the ceremony on the open ground of the longhouse, suddenly our spectator section collapsed. All of a sudden we—she and I—found ourselves holding each other in our shock and being squeezed together tightly in the crush of the other spectators. The beginning of an acquaintance that was both funny and pitiful.

There's no definition that describes precisely the atmosphere of love. It can be felt much more with the heart and the soul. A blue thread binds two feelings in an intimate sublimity. Which keeps connected two separate bodies in happy combat. It's this odd mood that's always been with me these past days.

We came together in a proper balance. Each accepting the other. Surrendering and accommodating in an appropriate constancy. The parents on both sides even seemed to provide sufficient opportunities and the fragrant breeze of their blessings. Sometimes I would go and meet her at Kampung Bawo, more often feeling the intimacy nurtured between two hearts with mutual hopes.

By managing within the limits of freedom, we both enjoyed our days of flowers. We often sank into passion-drenched embraces. Giving and receiving. Our spirits full of melodies and songs. Nature was so wonderful in giving space for us to express our love. The night was so wonderful in providing all-enveloping darkness so that we were free to love under the moon, while watching the flickering stars. The wind was so wonderful in providing air that was chilly, making us embrace ever tighter. Warming body and soul. We were scorched in love's blazing fire. Scorched, body and soul burned to a crisp. We plunged into the sea of love. Gulped it in and fumbled in its deepest depths that were impenetrable and white. White! White! White! The world had become white and we came to again. Immediately, we swam back to ourselves. We were jerked awake. We had become children of nature. Independent and filled with challenges. Naïve but hot, like the rapids that pounded and flung water onto stony soil.

"Kakak doesn't have doubts about me?" Rie begged assurance.

"I will come again to ask for you," I said with certainty.

"Rie is afraid that Kakak will be disappointed. What you see is what you get."

"And what about your kakak himself?"

"Rie will give up everything. All possessions, riches, and whatever you see in me.

Her eyes were shining.

The sky above us smiled. The earth that we stood on was like velvet, soft and beautiful. The brush and bushes around us nodded. The leaves waved and beckoned. A pair of birds flew together, grazed by the end of the sky and then bathed in the fleeting clouds. Our hearts were laughing. A pair of birds storming the dusk.

4

Several longhouses needed to be repaired with planking. We cut down a meranti tree far upriver from the kampung. The meranti was just too big. We couldn't get it rolling down to the river. Had to make a trestle. The logs were placed on the trestle. A crowd of us dragged them to the river. What a neat sound the trestle made as it bumped along on the wooden slipway. *Kletik! Kletek! Kletik! Kletek!* Everyone kept pulling to commands and accompanying laughter. The logs finally arrived on the bank and one by one were dropped into the river. *Byuuuur!* as each hit the water. Everyone cheered and yelled. But bad luck! The wasps were mad because their nests had been destroyed. Stung the trestle pullers. People went running off wildly and one of those wasps managed to sting my lip. Very painful. My lip swelled and went red, a real sight. Everyone burst out laughing again.

The logs were washed down by the current to the longhouse. Dragged up to Uncle Kiso's sawmill. The kampung men took turns sawing them into planks. Others prepared the equipment and concoctions for the nalin taun. Erected a special structure called a *serapo*, like a long shed, and made sitting platforms and racks. Two kinds of balian were invited. Balian *lawangan* and balian *bawe*, this second one for a special balian ceremony performed by a woman: the long and costly *timeq* ritual.

5

The moment a baby is born a balian must perform the *ngejakat* ceremony. When his umbilical cord dries and is removed, another rite is held, the *tempong pusong*. If the baby reaches its fortieth day, it must be bathed with unboiled river water. That is the *ngenus* ceremony. As its age progresses, the ceremonies go on longer and require large payments and considerable time.

When the child is ready to learn to walk, there is a ceremony whereby he or she is let down to the ground, *turun tana* is its name, when the child's feet touch the ground. Then comes the final ritual, the symbolic release from the straits of childhood, the *meles* ceremony, that is, when children are about five or six years old. From this time on, the child has entered a wide and complex world. A world filled with honey and flowers, with obstacles and challenges! Children will quickly sense their maturity when they use their independence in the midst of nature, in the midst of a world that is harshly challenging.

If the child is a boy, at the age of twelve, he will have separated a plot of his own from the huma of his parents. For that, the ritual of *peles tana* is performed to placate the earth god, Tonoy, when, for the very first time, he cuts down little trees to make his own huma. The kampung folk join in, help with cutting and felling big trees, burning them and planting rice. At rice-planting time, the *ngasek* ritual is held. The men will dig a hole in the new field with a sharpened stick and clusters of rice seedlings are inserted into the hole by women. Those seeds are then allowed to grow by themselves. Topsoil and the remnants of the ash become fertilizer, and the rice will burst into the open and grow in luxuriance.

A little hut to provide shade while watching the huma, called a *dangau,* will be built in the middle of the field. After the rice has grown for about two months, the women will pull out the grass and weeds in between the rice plants. At this time, the men of the longhouse have the chance for *berahan*, to look for resin and rattan in the forest. That's because the field work has now moved into the hands of the women.

When the plants began to be "pregnant" with fruit, a ritual for the god of the earth and the goddess of the rice will be performed. The final ceremony for the huma is when the rice harvest begins. Each type of young rice is taken little by little, some to be made into fried crisps called *emping*, and some to end up as cooking rice by being first fried and then pounded in a mortar. Cooked rice made from the young fruit of the fields is extremely fragrant, boiled first in a wok-like pan called a *kuali* with pre-boiled water. This rice is "stiff" but tasty, especially if eaten while still hot with side dishes of fried river fish or roasted chicken. Spicy condiments, curries and cucumber, and steamed vegetable salad with peanut dressing are the companions of the rice that fill the stomach and make the sweat run.

Children, upon reaching adulthood, equip themselves with the requirements of social and domestic life. A woman learns to weave, cook, to dress up, run a home, and about furniture and utensils, the adornments to complete herself with clothing and bedding, earrings that dangle, bracelets, and even how to apply lipstick. She has to know how to weed the huma, to harvest the rice, how to fish with a pole, split firewood, and draw water from the river. Males learn how to plait bamboo, make mats, the plaited bags known as *anjat*, to gather forest products, hunt, climb the log stair into the longhouse, set snares for animals, to work the huma dry rice fields, to build a house and learn *adat besara*, adjudication by adat law. All such preparations greatly influence and benefit them when they enter the world of household life, for marriage is one of life's challenges. And thus, when young people are brave enough to enter the married state, it means that they have matured and have completed their study of life and this existence.

6

When I was very small, I loved to set into the Melengén River the fish traps of wire netting and bamboo we call *bubu*. That river is shallow, clear in a reddish way. Perhaps because its springs come from swamps at its southern head. Fish straying into the bubu have scales that are reddish in color as well. After being cooked their taste differs from fish of the big river with its murky waters beside the longhouse. Such fish are rather sweet and rich-tasting when fried.

Kids my age fought with each other to lay the bubu into the streams of that river. Every morning and evening when the bubu was lifted up, they had caught quite a lot of fish. And this activity only stopped when a cobra got into Sengkay's bubu. He thought it was an eel. He released it from the bubu. Suddenly the snake bit him on the hand. He shrieked and we took off in fright. A snake shaman then saved his life. Astonishingly, the snake that bit him came of its own accord and kissed the wound on the victim's hand. Stuck out its tongue, stiffened and died. Sengkay lived. Since then we were cured of setting out any more bubu.

When the dry season arrives the rivers become shallow. The receding water line reveals white sand on the sloping banks. As kids, we often played on this sand. Boys and girls. No one was scared of falling prey to the crocodiles. We'd run far, all along the sandy bank, sometimes plunging into the river, chase each other around, or collect coal. Yeah, there was lots and lots of coal in this river! Coal was great for cooking and driving mosquitoes away!

A childhood bright and sunny. One time I played bride-and-groom. With Meta. The children welcomed us with cheers. Potok officiated. Several witnesses, two pairs of boys and girls, acted as our parents. A solemn and reverent ceremony.

When the ceremony was almost over, the longhouse suddenly started shaking. The panicked children ran off in every direction. The longhouse felt as if it would crumple from turning about in some supernatural hand. Twisting and turning, back and forth. Here and there creaking and breaking, plates smashing, with every part of the longhouse violently shaken.

"O gods! We fear the final day, do not pour calamities on our heads. We don't mean to make you angry. We are only filling the sweet moments in the breaks between ceremonies. We didn't mean to blaspheme, and didn't mean to set off your anger!" I made this plea silently.

Girls cried and sobbed. Pigs and chickens were running loose under the longhouse. The trees swayed. Everything around us rocked and shook in spasms until, without realizing it, Meta and I had just fallen into each other's arms. When everything subsided, we gingerly opened our eyes. She smiled, I smiled, the children cheered. My face felt so hot!

Oh gosh! That damned earthquake created a sweet event that I've never forgotten. Now most of the little pals of my childhood days have families of their own. Meta herself has two children.

I feel something tugging in my chest. My simple and innocent childhood has long gone. I just stagger and shuffle along by myself.

Enveloped in loneliness!

7

My father had a plot of rattan trees that was quite broad, several plots of rubber trees that were not particularly well tended, and groves of oil seed and fruit trees. But all of these failed to provide satisfactory returns because of inadequate communications infrastructure and poor management. The land in this region was fertile enough, and, during good seasons, durians hung on the high branches, the *langsat* trees were swollen with their little plum-like fruit, and the *rambutan* trees glowed with their red offerings like giant bonfires. The branches swayed and bent under the weight of their fruit. Such a shame! In the end these fruits just fell by themselves, uneaten by the longhouse people. Forest pigs and other wild animals wandered about eating the fallen fruit. Durian and cempadak fruit fell to the ground rolling and came to rest against one another. Cardamom, long durians, and our Kalimantan mango all rotted away here and there. The fruit rotted! Like the hearts and souls of rotten humanity!

The wild animals got fat. Pigtailed monkeys, leaf monkeys, pigs, deer, mousedeer, porcupines, and pangolins. The animals had children and their children had children. The polecat didn't steal chickens. The squirrel didn't gnaw on coconuts, the civet didn't eat the coffee beans. They looked for fruit in the gardens or in the forests.

This year there wasn't much of a fruit season. The croplands were overrun with pests. Rats and pigs made short work of the growing rice. The young cassava stalks were shorn of their leaves by the deer. Porcupines gnawed at the sugar cane. The fields were not safe and the kampung folk were jittery! These were catastrophes that had to be warded off by a nalin taun. Cleanse themselves, the soil, and the longhouse from defilement and all disgrace. Offer thanksgiving to the gods.

8

"If we cut across to the north from here," Rie said, "before noon we'll arrive at another waterfall."

I observed the direction she was pointing to. There was a footpath that twisted and turned like a gigantic snake slithering into the forest. "The waterfall is scary. High and straight down. Then it dives one kilometer into the earth. Do you want to go there?"

I shook my head.

"It's called Cavity Falls."

"Because the water goes into a deep hollow?" I asked.

"Good guess!" she replied with a laugh.

"You shouldn't praise a man." I looked at the rocks and at the treetops that were quietly swaying. "In case you get lost in a forest where only cross-dressers live."

Her expression didn't change. From the rocky heights we looked at the waterfall before us. Its waters frothed in whitening clots, one mass after the other impatiently waiting its turn. Then broke up the rocks below. Which were carried away and fell onto the shelves farther down. Finally, the riverbed sloped down, turned and its water looked calm.

"This life is like water." My thought suddenly revealed itself.

"It flows on and on." Rie interrupted my sentence that was slow in continuing. "It's up to us to give content and meaning."

Her words penetrated deeply. Like meditation focused on a high mountain or a river that flowed though boundless lowlands.

Rie? I was happy with her honest and open character. This was one girl who was intelligent and capable. Graceful in a natural simplicity. Her thoughts often flew out with unexpected sharpness. Stunning how she implanted her convictions. Her words, her movements and actions often aroused an inexplicable enchantment in me. A craving. There was between us the pure affinity in temperament, desires, and pleasures that links hearts in an inextricable bond.

"But nature controls us too much." My words sounded despairing. "We depend too much on it."

"We can change it," replied Rie forcefully.

"With dreams?" I mocked.

"With our minds," she mocked in return.

"We have minds, but we don't have the tools."

"Tools are built by the mind."

"For example?" I was testing just how far her thoughts would take her.

"Usually men know best." Rie had me truly cornered. "Especially if the man is ready to become a husband…"

We gazed at each other in silence. The water fell. Her eyes sparkled at me. Before us the thunder of the falling water. A neglected natural beauty. A gift of the Almighty, with never yet a human hand that could make it benefit life. Lots of people passing by would gaze at it, scrutinize it, turn away from it, or be indifferent to it. Damn it all! Lots of people considered this natural wonder a holy place!

In Kampung Bawo—the name "Bawo" means "mountainous region"—the views of nature are famed for their beauty. Hills rise up here and there, rivers of moderate width yawn and twist through gaps in the rocky mounts to sink into the horizon. There are many rapids and cascades at their headwaters. Like the one before us. Its name is Inar Falls, after a tragic girl. And there are many other waterfalls as well: Encepm, Lagey, Mapan, Sewet, Lungau, Gemuruh, Liwir, Menarung, among others. All of them are charming and could be put to use, if anyone had the ability, expertise, and capital.

"Let's dam this river upstream," I said, my voice startling Rie out of our long silence.

"What for?"

"Well," I said mockingly, "so you don't let your thoughts just hang around the kitchen." She made a grumpy face, but apparently wasn't offended.

"So?"

"We'll channel the water into the fields. Those dry fields we'd change into wet rice fields, huma into *sawah*.

"But we'd kill the waterfall. We wouldn't be able to gaze upon its beauty again."

"It wouldn't be dead. In fact it will be of use to us. We'd control its water. Over there we'll build a mill."

"A mill?"

"Where the people here would crush and pound the harvested rice."

"But I prefer to do this in the village mortar," Rie laughed, "really late in the afternoon or early in the morning. We don't have to line up then."

Her look was directed straight at me. Clear and fascinating, like a deep lake. The sun was rising. Its rays played between us through the swaying leaves as the wind pounced on them. The two of us had been tramping about this area since morning.

"You're fishing or seeing to the traps," Rie continued with her own hopes and dreams, "while our children are playing or sleeping, and I'll be able to winnow the rice I pounded the day before. We needn't save a lot of it because it'd go bad and not taste good." She chattered on and on like a magpie.

I kept on thinking about that dam and the water mill. If I could succeed, their advantages could change the way the kampung people thought.

"I thought you could support my views," I said in a voice that begged approval.

"Of course, there's no need to argue over it." Her hand pulled on my arm. "But this would need help and lots of sacrifice."

"Cooperation and mutual assistance are the main strengths of our society." I sounded like a preacher. "If anyone gets something going, our people become involved for sure. The elders will give their support and the youngsters will definitely join in if the older people bring them to work together."

"Also, being certain about the truth of those personal dreams," Rie offered a new thought. "You've got to stay strong carrying out this work, in case you get attacked by unexpected events."

We kept ambling along through that area. An excellent place, the soil looked fertile and easy to channel the water when the dam construction was underway. I was convinced such an undertaking would succeed, because the roots of mutual assistance were an unbeatable capital in society here.

I softly planted my lips on her brow in parting. The day before we had spent the entire day in our intimacies. We had linked promises in the middle of nature. Under the sky. Under the trees. Nature was witness. All of nature was witness. The sun was witness. The birds were witness. Two youths had fused their love through life and through death in the midst of the soughing wind, together with the thundering of their hearts and the voice of the falling water. In the innermost part of our souls, we both vowed one choice. To give of our entire selves. To bind two bodies in a spiritual unity.

Before her parents, I pledged sincerity to adat, filial devotion and my esteem. Our relationship had to be bound in a valid and proper way according to the prevailing rules of adat. An official envoy would come from my side to propose marriage to Rie within a time frame we had determined.

I had prepared the various items required for the official proposal. My mother sent fabrics and clothes for her future daughter-in-law. And kitchen knives, bracelets, hanging earrings, necklaces, shampoo in the form of a certain root with foaming properties, and the like. Our entire kampung welcomed all this with happiness.

But that was a month ago, and now I had been dashed onto sharp rocks. It's like having been flung out of a dream world. The thing happened so suddenly. Like a meteor, like the fireworks rocket that flares for just a moment and then vanishes forever without leaving a trace behind.

The days of the ninth month in our region are bright. The sky is always blue and the clouds thin. The wind is rarely strong, it just caresses softly with each of its breaths, swaying the leaves here and making them wave there. Just as it strokes the leafy cassava and waves my shirt drying on a line in front of the field hut.

I was exhausted. I had cut down a few trees which were now piled up in front of the hut. I lay down to take a break. The sun was at its very zenith. Unexpectedly a voice addressed me.

"What, alone?" Rie was on the ladder.

Before I had a chance to say a word, she attacked me greedily. Strange, it was as if I lost consciousness and simply dissolved. We wrestled on and on in a heat-stricken two-ness. I did everything that had happened between us previously. She was so hot and aroused. Passionate, very passionate.

And we drank in heavenly waters to slake our arid thirst. We fused together. We murmured and gasped when it all came. It lasted. And lasted! We fondled each other. Hearts and souls spoke wordlessly. We drank and drank again insatiably, until every joint had been totally sapped by fatigue. Face to face at the end of the final exhaustion. I saw Rie now utterly pale. Pale! But before I could ask, her mouth had crushed my lips. We were a long time like that. At the very peak, I felt how very cold her lips had become.

"I have long been dead!" Her face whitened and she staggered off.

I never had a final glimpse of her.

I was out cold.

9

The nalin taun ceremony had been underway for eight days. On the sixteenth day, a white water buffalo was to be slaughtered as a *peles* from Uncle Ningir, an offering to placate gods such as Tonoy. On the twenty-fourth day, another buffalo would be slaughtered as a sacrificial offering by the village folk to the gods. A vow that was in nature more of a supplication that in the years to come, they would receive adequate yields and sustenance. That the croplands would no longer be infested by vermin, bad luck would vanish, death would keep its distance, births would increase and happiness would blossom all the more among family members.

This ceremony was divided into three areas: within the longhouse interior, at the *serapo*, and at the riverbank alongside the longhouse. In each part, even numbers of pigs and chickens had to be sacrificed and even-numbered amounts of bamboo-cooked sticky rice had to be made.

At certain points in the ceremony, the music was accompanied by the gong-and-drum *buntang* music. The balian chanted mantras. Day and night they chanted these, addressing every deity, male and female, in the heavenly kingdom. The balian related all the events and accidents that had befallen the people in the longhouse. Then the gods were invited to visit the people on earth during the ritual. Every god and goddess was provided with the offerings appropriate to their tastes and status. The water gods were given offerings of fish and animals that come from the water. The earth deities, those of the skies, the gods of the air and others received prayerful homage according to their origins. You can't get any of this wrong! But the main tributary offering, the chickens, pigs, water buffalo, and the sticky rice have to be offered in a proportional way.

In the intervals between the chanting of the balian, there were dance performances. The form of these presentations changed every night. Now there was a performance of the gantar dance.

The music of the plucked strings pitched and rolled gently, its rhythm calm and slow. The dancers standing ready in the middle of the veranda. With both hands they held the dance accessories. At the forefront stood Ifing. It looked as if she would be their leader.

This dance portrayed the welcoming of a war chief newly returned from battle. A male youth dressed in magnificent war gear with all the decorations and ornaments appeared in the middle of the arena. Not a single one of his soldiers lived to come home, but they had managed to destroy the enemy longhouse. All his fighters had been hemmed in by fire. They had been caught in the trap set by the enemy who had carried out scorched-earth tactics against their own longhouse. It was in grief and sorrow that the unfortunate war chief had escaped and straightaway returned.

Such a wonderful dance! Only, I didn't quite agree with such a performance being presented in this sort of gleeful and cheery atmosphere. Wouldn't it have been more appropriate to select an episode of love or themes of home life rather than staging such sadness?

I was busy working through my own thoughts. Often spoke to myself and held internal question and answer sessions. Unaware that the play had ended with the commander meeting again with his sweetheart. So melancholy! Because that commander had just been relieved of his position. But his faithful lover still accepted him, even though he was now without position or office and facing destitution.

This performance jolted awake my recollection of Rie. My queen of the stage was really and truly gone. Was it because her fate was written with such a bad ending? Twice my love had ended with death. Rie fell together with two of her friends into the waterfall where I had dreamed of building a dam and a mill to pound rice. None of the three could be saved. Two of them were bruised and broken when swept away from the heights. Strangely, Rie wasn't damaged in the slightest. Her visage did not indicate pain, and there was even a faint smile still showing on her face and cold lips.

Had she killed herself? No! I wasn't sure. There hadn't been the least little rift between us. Was she taken by the water god? No! I don't believe that. Is there even such a thing as a water god? Maybe there is. But I am still not sure if he had it in him to snatch Rie's life away. That girl was just too good. Trusting and innocent. Or is it the guiltless who've got to become death's fodder?

My thoughts were running all wild. Several other dances began and ended. I wasn't paying much attention. The longhouse stayed noisy and bustling. I fell off to sleep in the midst of it all.

10

The nalin taun ceremony was now over. The visitors, the salung, had all gone home. The land and the forest had been placated with offerings of the blood of the animal sacrifices. The longhouse

residents were cleansed with offerings of *burey*, the mixture of rice
flour and sacral "flower water", and the blood of a chicken and a
pig and a buffalo. The gods were also presented with offerings. Not
one was left out. Sitoy was elevated to the same degree as Uncle
Ningir. I had to now address her as Aunt Sitoy.

Traces of this ceremony remained in the shape of the ritual
devices and accessories still scattered around the longhouse.
Loneliness welled up around us with the departure of the salung.
Several of the longhouse families had gone back to stay in their
huts to watch over the huma fields, and this added to the solitude
in the midst of the forest silence in this isolated inland region.

I participated in the cleansing. Rid myself of the harassment of
ugly shadows. Released my spirit from the oppression of the souls
of the dead.

I don't quite believe it, but in this region, things like what I had
experienced with Rie often occurred. Making love again after one
of the two had died was considered normal. The sweetheart who
had died before reaching the married state must inform the other
when it so happens that they are in different places. Only, for me,
this wasn't believable and I was completely unprepared to accept
it as fact. Something I considered extraordinary, very painful.
Spiritually frightening and medically disgusting. Even someone
we loved with all our heart. Received in a bizarre state. Something
like that makes you feel you're betraying yourself.

Is this the way life really is? That's what I asked myself. Only the
cycle of ceremony, one following right after the other? Or is this
life, in and of itself, in fact a ceremony?

So, what's the point of it all? Come. Exist. Then go. Lost without
a trace. Is that what we call life? If not, then what do we call life?
But if it is, what then?

11

"Kakak's daydreaming?" greeted Ifing as she passed by. She went straight into her bilik in the longhouse. I had no chance to reply. Surprised and speechless.

After that sad event that had separated me from her older sister, Waning, I never paid much attention to her. She appeared only fleetingly in the registry of my memories. A girl fast growing into her adolescence. Her figure was filling out nicely. She had a look about her that was no less fetching than her departed sister's. Word had it she had been proposed to a few times already, but she wasn't interested. Even foreigners had chased after her and given her lots of presents and souvenirs. But she kept refusing them.

More recently, I had been paying her closer attention. Her adolescence was blossoming into a true perfection. Her gentleness and movements, presence and character, all reminded me of Waning. She possessed a balance between her physical growth and her spirit. The moment we studied each other, her attitude towards me didn't change. Familiar, but maintaining the kind of distance a younger sister would keep from her older brother. It was tough for me to guess what was really in her heart.

In this I was certain: I was the one who always hesitated. Usually a girl would just wait. The boy had to make the first move. But because of my loss, I made no effort to launch an attack. Perhaps because we were too close, our eyes closed to many new things. That was her way, once a little girl whom I had seen when she was still running around naked. Even when she came of age, I never got around to drinking in her beauty. My feelings toward here were no more than that of a protective older brother, to the point that I worried that if I behaved strangely, out of line, she would paint me as a jackal. Greedy, pitiless, and a killer by choice.

"Actually, Kakak himself is the snooty one." Ifing glanced at me from the corner of her eye. She was really pretty when she was embarrassed like that. Her words were uttered in a hopeful tone that she disguised. "I'm sure the moment's soon arriving. And someone is going to come to me with words of love."

"Who?" I asked, curious.

"Just take a guess. Ifing is sure Kakak has known for a long time." Her face was one big grin, the way it always was with her. Pale. Natural. Within whom was stored the charm of a wise woman.

"I don't know," I said, perfectly honestly, "and, by the way, I am no fortune teller."

Hurt her feelings maybe, but she didn't say anything. Just walked off. While my thoughts still jumbled round and round.

All day long I asked myself: Who was the young guy that this cutie was waiting for? Was it me? Or no one at all? Maybe she was just blowing smoke at me. But why hadn't she accepted even one of those proposals? The conclusion was, she had to have had someone, someone in reserve. Me? Not possible! Our hearts had never taken soundings of each other. Our acquaintance was limited and formal. But who knows the heart of a woman? She's free to beam her smiles in every direction. But her heart? Her love? Decent women in our region tend to give their heart to just one man. The man they love. And who was the man that this girl loved? One happy guy, because a girl who truly wanted to be devoted and loyal, yearned for him. Like a natural mother, like tears that gush forth forever, like a mother hen that flaps her wings for her brood. But would he understand this?

In these uncertain moments, the knot separating us finally unraveled. After the loss of her older sister, she had promised herself never to let any boy into her life unless I was that one. I was jolted by unexpected thoughts that opened new possibilities on the pages of my calamity-smeared life. Whose cover had been wrapped with misery, suspicions and worries about the future.

"It would hurt if Ifing learned Kakak was going to propose to a Bawo girl. It would mean that I'd live in lonely solitude forever. As a younger sister who loves, I am determined and I pray. Waning is no more. May Kakak find happiness with another girl that he truly loves." A long string of mournful sentences. I saw her teardrops fall.

"But we won't be separated." I wiped away those tears. "Tears are no good on the face of a pretty girl."

We hugged.

A brief period of a love. During which we probed and took soundings of each other, rejected and gave. In the end, became one in the same longing: togetherness on the bridal floor of the longhouse. That was the ending which was the beginning of a departure for the new life we planned. In which, really and truly, ever since raw babyhood, the fingers of our love have been linked by the Being who is the Great Love.

V

Pelulung: The Marriage Ceremony

1

The temporary gate for the visitors was festooned with flowers of all kinds and colorful young coconut fronds. The colors came from mixing finely pounded plants and flowers, which were then cooked until thick and strong-hued. Even though the leaves had dried and had become fragile, their colors held and hadn't faded at all. Seen from afar, the multicolored leaves were gleaming and lustrous, swayed and caressed in the changing winds.

The way through the gate was blocked by the *ompong* ritual. This ceremony completely closed off the road and was divided into eight rows. On each row were placed items of a value in accordance with the status of the bride and groom, because each of these ceremonies calls for reciprocity. The more antique, old-fashioned and expensive the object displayed, the heavier the weight to be borne for the person who assumes it. For every ompong acceptance is exactly like acknowledging a debt. The emotional and financial burden bears down on the shoulders by an adat that demands continuity.

The visitors' gate was formed as an archway and faced the river bank landing where they would arrive. The length of the road to the landing was adorned with clusters of embellished palm fronds and flowers that were hung from fine strings of rattan. And right from the edge of the landing, along both sides of the road to the open space in front of the longhouse, hung *umbul-umbul*—long pennants and flags of brightly patterned cloth attached to the tops of poles.

Balai-balai with pavilions had been constructed where the road began, right at the edge of the open space, where visitors could rest. Usually, after passing through ompong, the guests would shake off their fatigue while enjoying the *loak* singing of the young boys and girls.

At times like this, loak are conventionally prescribed spoken exchanges, a questioning in song of the intentions of the arriving visitors. And according to the oldest adat tradition, the nature of these formulas requires responses. Representatives of the visitors have to relate the purpose of their coming. Only at the conclusion of this ritual welcome are the travelers invited to go up into the longhouse.

Inside the longhouse the guests were greeted with the cheerily rhyming *deguq* triplet verses and antiphonal *dongkoy* songs in their honor.

2

The ompong ceremony was concluded yesterday. Crowds of visitors came from the southern villages. This time, the ritual was the most expensive and grandly performed because our parents wanted it that way. Ifing's father was our village headman, but he had been an outsider, having been born south of here. Therefore, the ones counted as outside visitors and upon whom the debt of ompong was imposed were those southerner *salung*, Ifing's family.

The rites were very splendid. Both the welcome ceremony at the head of the road and the one inside the longhouse. The deguq and dongkoy antiphons linked the voices of the joyous boys and girls in call and response. This was followed during the night with the *ngelengot* ceremony, when stories were told in song. An aggressive kind of song in which opponents tried to defeat each other with metaphors and symbols. The very best of the ngelengot performers are mostly old people, highly skilled at concealing the meanings and secrets of language.

And of course there was the gantar dance. Several girls and boys bowed and swayed in the dance that described the friendship between two villages as an intimate relationship. Intermittent performances made the night pass by very quickly.

"Behave as calmly as you can," advised Kak Usuk as she went on bathing me. "Don't look pale or shaky."

"Yeah," I said absentmindedly. I was out wandering with my thoughts. Drifting like the wind over the broad world.

A pure and natural marriage means the spiritual and physical union of two people. They exist, live, and breathe. Have children who have children. Then they get old and die. And after death, what? Eternal life?

"You must look and behave elegantly, like a god." Kak Usuk scattered my thoughts in their endless round.

"And if she does not look elegant like a goddess?" I was taken aback by the tone of my own question.

"But she *is* a goddess. Your love goddess!"

Kak Usuk was finished with neatening and arranging everything that went on my head. She arranged my wedding clothes with the utmost care. She checked every corner and fold again and again until everything looked just right.

"Of course she's a goddess. But I'm no god." I tried to lose the nervousness that was making me shake all over.

"You're a god. She's a goddess. You're perfect together," said Kak Usuk. Her praise went on and on. She was actually my cousin, the one who watched over me the most. And, since I was an only child, I felt that she was my real older sister. As a sign of her affection toward me, when I was little, she once gave me a hundred rupiah.

The men of this region are mighty and forceful. They have to pit themselves against nature. The women of this region are valiant and courageous. They give birth to the children of nature. But nature challenges them. They're ready to lose or to win. "Waning was beaten by nature," I reflected.

"Rie returned to the womb of nature." This thought stabbed into me. But it was no good to keep turning that sad event over and over in my mind. I killed my own thought. "This is now your day of happiness," I thought calmly. A man must subdue nature. Like those foreigners. Many meranti trees have been brought crashing down. Keruing trees turned into logs. Pulled to the river, and then carried down by the current to who knows where? They won. Rich and bountiful nature surrendered. Our rich and bountiful nature surrendered!

"Barren! Barren!" The words exploded from my mouth just like that. Like in a delirium.

"I've told you, be calm, be calm…. You'll come across gloomy and moody if you can't control yourself," said Kak Usuk with a worried look.

"I was thinking of all those meranti," I quickly explained.

"Meranti?" Kak Usuk didn't quite follow me.

"Won't our region become barren and dried up if the meranti keep getting cut down willfully and unaccountably? Thousands of little trees come down with them and die. In time this island of ours will be turned into a desert, like the Sahara or the Gobi. Dryness torments. Floods no longer follow their seasons. And from a desert, our region will turn into a sea!" My words shot forth like arrows in leaping pursuit of their prey. Keen and spirited. As if emanating from an agitator's megaphone.

"There's always something going on with you." Kak Usuk only now grasped what I had said.

"This is an important fact, hey! The boundaries of our dry croplands are always under pressure."

Kak Usuk kept fixing the parts that weren't quite right yet.

"In the end, we will be driven out. Forced out of this region. We will become forest wanderers." My bitter words vomited out without waiting for a reply.

"Today is your marriage day. You have the right to taste the happiness of just the two of you in these moments," advised Kak Usuk quietly.

"That's just it!" My emotions grew more and more heated and unruly. "My descendants need to eat. The forests here have been shaved bare. The ancient forests have turned into abandoned young forests. In the end, it will be overgrown with brush and barren wasteland. We won't be able to cultivate huma. Erosion will wash away the soil. Flooding will be unavoidable."

Kak Usuk kept on fixing and arranging.

"We'll work the huma when it floods?" I was getting hotter all the time.

"Of course not. They say there'll be reforesting."

"What they say is always nicer than the way it is. The reality is different. They simply walk away from their clear-cuts. Use them, then toss them! The forests and the women, abandoned just like that. Like garbage. Despised. They run off and hug other women, tear down new areas."

Kak Usuk worked on the parts that were not yet perfect. The music on the veranda was being struck in the *buntang* rhythm. An errand boy brought notice that the ceremony was just about to start. The bride was all ready. I looked over my own costume. Its arrangement was completed, and slung nicely.

My room was just like Ifing's, outside the longhouse itself and constructed in the form of a royal bower, called *jayung*. During the ceremony, the groom is escorted by boys, while the bride, by girls. They both are to meet at the veranda, and where all the appurtenances of the ritual have been made ready. The elders were waiting there, including the village headman who would perform the marriage blessing.

3

The marriage date had been planned eight months before. A healer had chosen the very best moment of the very best day. A day considered to possess mystical power. It had to be right at the full moon and the performance of the ceremony could not go beyond the mid-day hour.

I was now twenty-one years old and Ifing was seventeen. A fine gap of years for a marriage, because usually a woman's physique shrinks faster than a man's. If the ages are too close, the woman will look much older, and normally for men at a certain age, their youth will revive, while the woman will not be up to this. Without a proper release, men weak in their faith will go the crooked road. This was one of the problems taken into account for my marriage. In addition to the kinship factor, because of the failure with Waning, whose life had been snatched from her, it was natural that she should have been replaced by Ifing, her younger sister. And our parents of course wanted it that way. I was the one person unable to recognize the signs of love hidden in the heart of a young woman like Ifing. The calamity that struck Rie just aggravated my wound.

"Does Kakak really and truly choose me?" asked Ifing, her head bowed. Just as her older sister had done, the one who was now gone.

I nodded.

"Not just a place of refuge?" She continued to look down. Sparrows pecked at the young rice on their shoots. "Ifing worries that Kakak is only running away after being hit twice by calamities."

"I chose you. I don't want misfortune."

I sought her eyes.

The heavens scintillated. The wind soughed through the underbrush. The tree stumps were pensive.

"No! No!" She suddenly sprung straight up, ready to move away. I grabbed hold of her hand.

"What is it?"

"Doesn't Kakak belong to that Bawo girl?" She asked, her jealousy flaring. "Now let go of me!"

I held her arm tightly.

"No!"

She struggled to break free. Tears seeped from her eyes. A strange wildness flashed across her face.

I couldn't bear seeing her like that.

Finally, she relaxed. I wiped away her trickling tears.

I sat her down again. Like before.

"If you really don't want me…" I jumped up. But as fast as I was, she pulled my arm even faster.

"What can I do?" I said sharply.

"No way! No way!" she sobbed.

"So then, Ifing can't accept me?"

"I'm so hurt from loving you too much…" She wept with harsh choking sobs. "But…"

"But I've belonged to someone who is dead." My chest was slit open.

"No way! No way! No way!" she tugged at my arm. Her body shook all over. "No way!"

We stood there, the two of us, like actors in a sad play. The floor of the field hut creaked beneath our bare feet.

"Ifing will die young! The healer said that Ifing's going to die young!" She burst out weeping. Tears streaming down. "Like Kak Waning, Ifing will die young!"

"No!" I said firmly. "We will marry. Right away! There's no death! There won't be any death! We'll live a long life. Filled with happiness."

Suddenly we found ourselves in each other's arms. Ifing had been very affected by her sister's death. A few of her tears landed on my cheek. Warm. This girl was too sensitive.

"There's not a single person who can predict death. There isn't," I assured her. "The healer's no god."

Ifing, her expression happy. So pretty! Her bridal clothes extremely smart-looking. Wrapped around a very nice body. Angelic, elegant and enchanting. Her expression clear and pure. Not a drop of grief hung there.

The ceremony itself was rather long and tedious. There was questioning, sermons. There were blessings and much advice. I felt exhausted and drowsy.

After it was all over, the longhouse burst into an uproar of cheers and shouts. "Best wishes" expressed over and over. Our hands numbed by the numerous and prolonged greetings.

4

Groom? This was the moment I left my longtime solitary state. It would have been impossible for my natural youth to survive in tormented isolation.

Flowers had been scattered all over the surface of the bed. Their fragrance bit. The mat was pure white. The arrangements in the room were very, very nice.

Ifing had changed her clothes. She had been wearing a long lacey jacket. Her body was slim and graceful. Smiled at me, as her hand brushed off her skirt which wasn't dirty. She always acted the pampered girl. It showed from her movements and behavior. It showed from her words. From her face that enticed.

We rolled on the mattress. Meanwhile, out on the veranda the music flowed on as it accompanied the successive dancers. Toddies and other kinds of drinks and food during parties like this kept coming forth. This was the pleasantest and most enjoyable moment. When you eat, drink, and just let yourself go. Get totally smashed, barf or sprawl about, totally satiated.

Newlyweds? We had entered this world. According to adat, we had to stay shut up in the longhouse for three days. Our feet couldn't touch the ground. Certain appointed people would provide for our every need during that time.

For forty days, the new couple must be together. Paddle a sampan on the river together. Tread a small footpath together. Go into the fields together and return to the longhouse together. Or go pole-fishing or digging tubers or taro, cutting down bananas or rattan, and even paying a call on other longhouses. No matter where, they have to be together for forty days.

I pulled my wife into my arms. Everything had come to this. No more suspicions. No more any doubts about unfaithfulness between us. That's how close we were! Breath that was hurried. Bodies that sprawled. Life-souls that were one.

There was no more music. No more night. No more bed. No more wind. No more weather. No more! There was only the two of us! And we dove to the bottom of love. Groped and fumbled at depths unexpected. Rocked and swayed in a cradle that undulated and billowed. Reaching the wave's very peak, breathless. Gasping and panting. The delicious fatigue shrunk. Rain had fallen upon fertile earth, rain that was so, so heavy.

A real downpour.

5

We suddenly awoke from sound sleep. Like coming back from a long and distant journey. The sun was high and outside its rays shone everywhere. For a moment, we embraced and touched our cheeks together. We arose together and straightened out the blanket and the mat, wet from the previous night's rain. We both smiled. The day smiled. The earth smiled.

Very faintly on the veranda the old radio, the gift from Tuan Smith, played a song. The ending of the song was crystal clear. Grand and solemn.

"Great Indonesia, freedom! Freedom! My land, my country that I love. Great Indonesia, freedom! Freedom! Long live Indonesia!"

Instantly, the song ended. Then a piercingly loud voice could be heard as if wanting to rip up the world. The old radio stuttered and sputtered. I nudged Ifing. We both pricked up our ears. The ending sentence of the speech was sharp. Just like some slogan.

"God will not change the fate of a people before that people change their own fate!"

For a moment we gazed at each other. Then smiled to ourselves.

A Brief Note by the Author after the Passage of Thirty Years

Upacara (*Ceremony*) was the first long story I wrote. Thereafter, I wrote a few more long stories, among which those published were *Api Awan Asap* (*Fire Cloud Smoke*), *Wanita di Jantung Jakarta* (*Woman in the Heart of Jakarta*), *Lingkaran Kabut* (*Area of Haze*), *Bunga* (*Flower*), and *Perawan* (*Virgin*). Others are still in manuscript form—quite a few, dozens of titles. Some of these have been carried in serial form in several print media; however, they've never yet been published as books because they still need tight editing and—maybe even—additions or shortening of the manuscripts that have been finished. Among them as well are those that are still two-thirds finished, half-finished, a quarter finished. And there are some that are only looking for the best endings for appropriate conclusions.

Ceremony, *Fire Cloud Smoke*, and *Virgin* are novels written very quickly, in one week. The first chapter of *Ceremony* was written in just one day in Samarinda in 1974, when I was twenty-one years old, after I had finished research at the East Kalimantan Regional Development Bank for my thesis and was waiting to head back to Yogyakarta. That first chapter was later carried as a short story in the literary magazine *Horison* in 1975 (or was it 1976?). With the encouragement of Ragil Suwarna Pragolopati, that short story

Upacara, Korrie Layun Rampan, GRASINDO Gramedia Widjasarana Indonesia, Jakarta: 2007, pp vii-xi.

was developed into the first chapter of *Ceremony*. The following chapters were written over five days because I was racing to meet the deadline for the closing of the 1976 Jakarta Arts Council's Novel Writing Contest.

The funny thing about submitting the manuscript to that contest was that five copies of the manuscript had to be sent in. However, because I rushed to quickly send these off—actually, the deadline for submittal had already been exceeded, so that the postage stamp was backdated to the final day for sending—only three copies were actually sent in, requiring two copies to follow the next day. At the time of the 1976 Writers' Meeting, when HB Yassin announced the winner of the contest, I was at the Art Gallery (*Wisma Seni*)—and so did not directly hear the results of the announcement—rereading my copy of *Ceremony* that I had submitted to any publisher willing to publish the work of a beginning writer. I was amazed when I was greeted by the writer Nasjah Djamin who declared me the top winner, followed by S Sinansari Ecip (Makassar) and Ramadhan KH (who at that time had settled in Paris). Perhaps out of curiosity, startled, or never expecting that I would be the winner, Nasjah himself read the draft of *Ceremony* for a few moments and commented "Poetic!"

Naturally, I was very surprised and happy. I had never expected I could win with my draft messily typed in carbon copy, because I was speeding along and didn't have the chance to reread it. Moreover the contestants were for the most part dominated by senior literary figures, among them Suwarsih Djojopuspito, Putu Wijaya, Th. Sri Rahayu Prihatmi, Musytari Yusuf, Suparto Brata, Ragil Suwarana Pragolapati, Chairul Harun, and others, all of who made up a substantial total. On that day also, Emha Ainun Nadjib conveyed the message of Ajip Rosidi, the director of Pustaka Jaya, asking for a draft of *Ceremony* for publishing. At the time, Pustaka Jaya was the only private-sector publisher, the most courageous and serious in publishing literary works. Linus Suryadi AG and I walked from the Ismail Mazurki Park toward Jalan Kramat II, where the Pustaka Jaya office was.

My joy was complete after the daily *Suara Karya* carried it as a serialized story in 1977. In 1978, *Ceremony* was published as a book, and in less than a year the first printing was sold out. However, subsequently *Ceremony* had to wait twenty-two years before the second printing appeared, as it did in 2000.

From its first publication, this novel received a broad welcome from readers, literary critics, and academics as well as literature students of the final level who wrote on it for their dissertations at a number of universities and colleges throughout our country. That's why in this publication there has been not the slightest addition or deletion, other than a little editing of the punctuation, sentences, and misprints found in the previous two printings.

As a first novel, *Ceremony* was written as an experiment of my ability to learn and practice writing long manuscripts. Before that, I had only written poetry, short sketches, essays, and small-scale literary criticism suitable for newspaper and general magazine space. As it turned out, writing a novel requires stamina and primary abilities, particularly in the use of language, plot layout and narrative continuity.

Even though it was written in one week, actually the writing process was merely a transcription of a story that had been planned for decades. *Ceremony* is not a novel that was improvisational in its writing, but rather its composition was outlined as a blueprint with material adopted from the actual cultural reality. Thus, *Ceremony* is actually a realistic novel in that it takes its setting from the world of the Dayak people, a world that is exotic, magical, exciting and filled with ambiguities.

Thirty years on, when I reread *Ceremony*, I feel like a tide receding to past times, to the period of my childhood with all sorts of paraphernalia of ceremonies in countryside *kampung* that don't even appear as dots on the map. Realistically, what ended up being written in this novel, especially as it related to humans, the forest, the land, flora and fauna, was intensely affecting. Capitalism, colluding with Authority, and then hitching a free ride on modernization, has created chaos, because it has taken too much and in an excessively dehumanized way; and the Nusantara concept and even regional autonomy that followed it cannot fully contribute to repair and heal the lashings and welts that have already unleashed tears and blood. What remain now are only the furrows of the wounds and abrasions that erode and erode the shores of the river of life.

Sendawar, August 17, 2005
Korrie Layun Rampan

Foreword to the Original Indonesian Edition *)

This novel describes a spiritual experience that is internalized by the character "I" when undergoing various kinds of crisis rites organized by the inhabitants of a Dayak *kampung* community in the interior of Kalimantan. Different, successive rituals are depicted in this novel, beginning with the roaming of the protagonist's soul to Lumut (that is, Heaven) that takes place within a ceremony dedicated to his cure. This is followed by *balian* (shamanism) as it is linked with *nasuq juus*, the search for the lost soul—in this case, also that of the narrator/protagonist. Next, *kewangkey*, the ceremony for the burial of human bones, and *nalin taun*, an annual festival offering gifts to nature and the gods for warding off disaster from the kampung. And finally, the *pelulung*, or wedding, ceremony, wherein "I" enters the life stage of marriage after some years of "erotic adventures".

Rite after rite, event after event, all are described in symbolic language, dense with poetic rhythms and images. Its esthetic virtues would be lost if abbreviated and formulated in discursive language. For a grasp of the essence of the story, several excerpts sufficient enough to convey its beauty are provided here.

Sourced from Upacara, Korrie Layun Rampan, GRASINDO Gramedia Widjasarana Indonesia, Jakarta, 2007, pp xii-xx.
This foreword, written by Dodong Djiwapradja, was the responsibility of the jury for the novel-writing contest sponsored by the Jakarta Arts Council (Dewan Kesenian Jakarta) in 1976. The other members of the jury were HB Jassin, M Saleh Saad, Ali Audah, and Rusandi Kartakusuma.

The story begins with the depiction of "I" regaining consciousness, while an individual ceremony is being performed for his recovery:

> *Like suddenly awakening from deep sleep. Heavy, every part of me. My hands, my feet, everything stiff when I moved them. No energy at all.*
>
> .....
>
> *Mother let go of me and raised her face from my body when Uncle Tunding squatted beside me. The getang on his wrists clinked and jingled as he brushed the shredded banana leaves across my face. Then lowered these to my chest. There was a coolness in the touch of these fibers, the caressing of a wanton breeze.*
>
> *Only now did I realize that this balian ceremony was for me. What I didn't understand was why I felt in perfect health. But realizing the sumptuousness of the offerings, I knew that the patient now undergoing such a ritual must have arrived at the most critical stage. I couldn't care less! Instinctively, I shut my eyes tight as Uncle Tunding brought his final incantations to an end.*
>
> *Let's get this over and done with, now that another event is blocking my inner vision, roughly forcing my mind to bring to light that strange and truly wondrous event.*

Here, the description of the narrator-protagonist's soul being brought by his late grandfather to Lumut feels beautiful and compact:

> *"Yes, the beginning is strange. But a true man is always able to overcome obstacles. This is the road." He points. "Go alone. We will soon meet in a place not in this world. Be off now!"*

And, just like that, Grandpa himself disappears, like a wisp of smoke billowing into a chain of clouds in its ever-recreating composition.

In the balian ceremony, it feels like we are taken by "I" to join him in internalizing and instilling within us the universe and life of the Dayak people, as if we ourselves plunge into their mysterious world, their cosmos, their system of beliefs. Do they believe in the One Supreme God? The answer to this is conveyed in a conversation between Uncle Jomoq and Mr Smith. Mr Smith is an anthropologist who is carrying out research in the interior of Kalimantan. Moreover, he seems also to be a missionary who wants to introduce "the Savior" to the Dayak. But the Dayak reject this:

> *"I showed that foreigner that we have God," Uncle Jomoq continued. "Once with a crow. Once with a pigeon, and once with a hornbill. The man nodded, impressed."*
>
> *…*
>
> *"With so many gods, doesn't rivalry arise among them?" Tuan Smith asked.*
>
> *"Not at all. Because they have different places, positions, prestige, and powers. Like, for example, a government or military hierarchy. Each echelon has its own tasks and authority and rights."*
>
> *"So, is there a High God?"*
>
> *"Letala. He is the highest. The Creator."*
>
> *"And beneath him?"*
>
> *"Many, many. They are mentioned in the language of the healers, and given offerings, one after the other, and according to their ranking."*
>
> *"And if, for example, the lower gods rebel against the highest god?"*
>
> *"See, humans are always idealizing naïve thoughts. We always equate the instincts of the gods with the lusts of*

humans. Coups d'état never occur in heaven, because the gods do not possess lustful instincts."

"Heaven! What's that?"

"The house of eternity." Uncle Jomoq gazed deeply into the foreigner's eyes. They both looked at each other. The foreigner nodded.

"Is it like a palace, like a longhouse?"

"It is just like a kingdom. The highest god resides on Lumut as the center of heaven. The other gods occupy their places throughout the heavenly realm.

"And their subjects?"

"The spirits of people who win. The spirits of dead persons who were sent off to heaven in the tiwah and kewangkey ceremonies, their bones purified and put in their final resting place."

"And if those people had a lust for power?" persisted Tuan Smith.

"The world of the spirits is the one of immortality. All worldly instincts will have been cleansed. There are no physical cravings, because they went forward to greet the horizon of death. The inhabitants of Lumut exist in the world of life."

"Including the underling gods?"

"All the citizens of heaven and their subjects."

"The signs of being convinced of the divine truth?"

"Maintaining contact, making dedications and offerings, and healing rituals."

"What if the supreme god becomes old, feeble, and dies?" Tuan Smith gave him no quarter.

"In heaven there is no old age. There's no counting the years or consideration of age. Not like here on earth. Everything is fixed in newness for all time. Because there is no death in that place."

"Surely its inhabitants get bored in such a fixed state."
"Bored? Haven't worldly appetites all been rooted out?"
"If so, there's nothing there."
"The tree of life is there."
"The tree of life?"
"Like our bodies. The heart beats, the breath moves in
rhythm. All the members are bound together at the center
of unity. The body is the heaven that appears in our eyes."

Uncle Jomoq smiled in satisfaction with his explanation.
Tuan Smith and his companions kept nodding.

It is clear in this novel that ceremony constitutes the very center of Dayak life. Every individual, from babyhood to old age—even into death—must undergo ceremonies. Of course, after death, it is the family that organizes that ceremony. For example, the *kewangkey* ceremony, the ritual of burying human bones. "I", who seems to be consumed by modern civilization, makes this reflection in regard to that ceremony:

Is this the way life really is? That's what I asked myself.
Only the cycle of ceremony, one right after the other? Or is
this life, in and of itself, in fact a ceremony?

So, what's the point of it all? Come. Exist. Then go. Lost
without a trace. Is that what we call life? If not, then what
do we call life? But if it is, what then?

However, even though "ordinary life" seems only the interstices between ceremonies, in this novel, descriptions of it are presented in a very arresting way. While life is dense with ritual, "I" is again and again involved in sexual love. This begins with Waning, his first sweetheart. But disaster strikes. When "I" returns from wanderings in the forest, Waning is no more. A heartbreaking scene, when "I" discovers the last remaining articles of his lover, is conveyed most impressively:

Her weaving truly had been completed. Beautiful, so beautiful. There was embroidery that pictured our holy love. Our bridal clothes. Only the inner parts still awaited final refinement. But now it was all pieces in disarray. It couldn't be otherwise. Just let Waning take everything with her. I did not want those things becoming the burden of a memory that would just drag on and on.

Waning had gone home to the Deity and could never come back.

Everywhere was in twilight!

.....

On her water gourd were little scratches, a hundred and fourteen of them. A hundred and fourteen days I was gone after Waning took water with her gourd. On the one hundred and fourteenth day, the hungry crocodile devoured her. On the one hundred and fifteen day, I came. But Waning had gone on the morning of the previous day. Yes, just yesterday morning!

When certain ceremonies are held, there is dancing and singing, and among these girl singers, there is one who is their leader, a kind of prima donna, or *sripanggung*, to use the Indonesian term. Waning had been the sripanggung in one of the rituals. But Waning was now gone. And now Renta became the sripanggung. "I" then began going out with Renta. Renta goes away, to who knows where? The word is that she was taken away by a foreigner. "I" then meets Rie, a girl who also is the sripanggung in one of the ceremonies. "I" seems to discover his lost love in Rie. But as fate would have it, Rie also goes and never returns. During one of the ceremonies in which there is a presentation of dances, "I" recalls his lover, Rie:

This performance jolted awake my recollection of Rie. My queen of the stage was really and truly gone. Was it because her fate was written with such a bad ending? Twice my love had ended with death. Rie fell together with two of her pals into the waterfall where I had dreamed of building a dam and a mill to pound rice. None of the three could be saved. Two of them were bruised and broken when swept away from the heights. Strangely, Rie wasn't damaged in the slightest. Her visage did not indicate pain, and there was even a faint smile still showing on her face and cold lips.

Had she killed herself? No! I wasn't sure. There hadn't been the least little rift between us. Was she taken by the water god? No! I don't believe that. Is there even such a thing as a water god? Maybe there is. But I am still not sure if he had it in him to snatch Rie's life away. That girl was just too good. Trusting and innocent. Or is it the guiltless who have to become death's fodder?

Finally, the narrator-protagonist finds his *jodoh*, the match intended for him all along. Ifing, the younger sister of Waning, appears to have been secretly in love with him. Only then does he notice this sweet, cute girl. It turns out that Ifing has Waning's gentleness and prettiness. So, as the story ends, the ceremony to bind these two youths in union is held. Such a rite is called *Pelulung*.

The marriage date had been planned eight months before. A healer had chosen the very best moment of the very best day. A day considered to possess mystical power. It had to be right at the full moon and the performance of the ceremony could not go beyond the mid-day hour.

. . .

We stood there, the two of us, like actors in a sad play.
The floor of the field hut creaked beneath our bare feet.

"Ifing will die young! The healer said that Ifing's going to
die young!" She burst out weeping. Tears streaming down.
"Like Kak Waning, Ifing will die young!"

"No!" I said firmly. "We will marry. Right away! There's
no death! There won't be any death! We'll live a long life.
Filled with happiness."

Suddenly we found ourselves in each other's arms. Ifing
had been very affected by her sister's death. A few of her
tears landed on my cheek. Warm. This girl was too sensitive.

"There's not a single person who can predict death. There
isn't," I assured her. "The healer's no god."

In this novel, even though it stays centered on the ceremonies, other aspects of life are extensively covered as well. The problem of the arrival of outsiders in the interior of Kalimantan disturbs its inhabitants. Those foreigners bring calamity. They marry Dayak girls who are then just left behind, pregnant or the mothers of their children. All of this is felt to be disastrous and a ceremony is then performed. This is expressed in these deeply moving sentences:

All that was left were the children without fathers. All
that was left were the wives without husbands. The children
grew like the wild trees in the forest. Never knew from
which tree they had sprung.

In the minds of the kampung people, these events were
what caused so many calamities and deaths, such misery,
and such bad seasons, because the weather brought only
stinking wind and clouds. The rains that came were the
rains of disaster. The heat that radiated was a heat that
scourged. The people's nighttime songs were no longer as
sweet-sounding as they had been in the past. The voices

were quavery. Like lamentations. Like tears that stung. The wind brought weeping, the weather brought weeping. Weeping that went on and on. The weeping of the village, the weeping of the forest. The crying of children. The weeping of wives who locked up grief inside themselves.

In the dialogue below, their identity comes through very sharply. They question the presence of those outsiders. Besides leaving women pregnant or their newborn babies, those "foreigners" are also razing the forests. Great trees are cut down and then rolled down into the river. The leveling of the forest endangers the lives of the people of the interior in their agriculture.

"Nalin taun, there's no other choice," I heard Father say decisively. "A lot of bad things have hit our village, but we've just kept quiet. Don't all those things have to be cleansed so that our village can be cleansed? And us along with it?"

"And those outsiders, too," Uncle Lengur added. "We are guilty before the gods for giving in too much."

"They've also got to bear responsibility!" offered Kojok.

"It's no use our casting blame on others," Father continued. "The important thing is that we re-discover ourselves. That we become ourselves. Not other people. Especially when we're in an atmosphere of crisis, vulnerable even." He was a bit longwinded.

"But what's most troubling and humiliating for us are those foreigners," said Kojok stubbornly. "We're being taken advantage of in big way. The forest and the women."

"What's important in this discussion is, do we agree and are we able to hold a nalin taun or not? We aren't having anything to do with the foreigners!" insisted Father with words that brooked no opposition.

"At least we can ask for support." Kojok was rather deflated from his emotional flare-up.

"No need!" the other elders replied, almost with one voice.

"That'd be shameful! We're no beggars!" yelled Uncle Kedis.

"We are a mighty people. It's always been forbidden to go begging!"

There are so many excellent parts that could be cited, but I expect that these are sufficient to give a sense of how good this novel is. This is not a novel with a clear plot, although from the angle of structure it is quite good as a novel. The language employed is appropriate for the material being expressed. It is said in one of the modern theories, if literature is to survive it has to return to myth as the basis or source of its inspiration. I am of the view that *Ceremony* is a novel that can respond to that challenge. "Literature of the Absurd" finds it difficult to communicate with its public, most importantly because its source is not the myth of living together. Literature of the Absurd believes only in one's own personal self as an autonomous individual and not in humanity beyond oneself. I feel genuine literature must be able to foster belief in humanity, in the sense of "fellow humanity".

Dodong Djiwapradja
Translated by George A Fowler

Additional Reading Material

General

King, VT. *The Peoples of Borneo*, Oxford: Blackwell, 1993.

Sellato, B. *Hornbill and Dragon. Art and Cultures of Borneo*, Singapore: Sun Tree, 1992.

On the Benuaq

Couderc, P, & K Sillander (eds). *Ancestors in Borneo Societies. Death, Transformation, and Social Immortality*, Copenhagen: NIAS Press, 2012.

Crevello, SM. *Local Land Use on Borneo: Applications of Indigenous Knowledge Systems and Natural Resource Utilization among the Benuaq Dayak of Kalimantan, Indonesia*, PhD thesis, Louisiana State University, 2003.

Gönner, Christian. *Patterns and Strategies of Resource Use among the Dayak Benuaq of East Kalimantan, Indonesia*, PhD thesis, Albert-Ludwigs Universitaet, Freiburg, Germany, 2000.

Gönner, Christian. *A Forest Tribe in Borneo. Resource Use among the Dayak Benuaq*, New Delhi: DK Printworld, 2002.

Haug, Michaela. *Poverty and Decentralisation in Kutai Barat. The Impacts of Regional Autonomy on Dayak Benuaq Wellbeing*, Bogor : CIFOR, 2007.

Haug, Michaela. *Poverty and Decentralisation in East Kalimantan. The Impact of Regional Autonomy on Dayak Benuaq Wellbeing*, Freiburg: Centaurus, 2010.

Hopes, Michael. *Ilmu: Magic and Divination Amongst the Benuaq and Tunjung Dayak*, Jakarta: Puspa Swara & Rio Tinto Foundation, 1997.

Hopes, Michael, Dalmasius Madrah T, and Karaakng. *Temputn: Myths of the Benuaq and Tunjung Dayak*, Jakarta: Puspa Swara & Rio Tinto Foundation, 1997.

Knappert, SC. "*Beschrijving van de onderafdeeling Koetei,*" BKI *(Bijdragen tot de Taal-, Land- en Volkenkunde van Nederlandsch-Indië)*, 58: 575-654, 1905.

Massing, Andreas. "The Central Mahakam Basin in East Kalimantan: A Socio-Economic Survey," *Borneo Research Bulletin*, 18 (1): 64-100, 1986.

Sillander, Kenneth. "Local identity and regional variation: Notes on the lack of significance of ethnicity among the Bentian and the Luangan," *Borneo Research Bulletin*, 26: 69-95, 1995.

Sillander, Kenneth. *Acting authoritatively: How Authority is Expressed Through Social Action Among the Bentian of Indonesian Borneo*, PhD thesis, Swedish School of Social Science Publications, Helsinki: University of Helsinki Press, 2004.

Tromp, SW. "*Een reis naar de bovenlanden van Koetei,*" *Tijdschrift voor Indische Taal-, Land- en Volkenkunde*, 32: 273-304, 1889.

Weddik, AL. "Beknopt overzigt van het Rijk van Koetai op Borneo," *Indisch Archief*, 1 (1): 78-105; 1 (2): 123-160, 1849-50.

On Ceremonies

Bonoh, Yohannes. *Belian Bawo*, [Samarinda]: Propinsi Kalimantan Timur, Proyek Pengembangan Permuseuman, 1984-85.

Bonoh, Yohannes. *Lungun dan Upacara Adat*, [Samarinda]: Propinsi Kalimantan Timur, Proyek Pengembangan Permuseuman, 1984-85.

Dalmasius Madrah T. *Lemu. Ilmu Magis Suku Dayak Benuaq & Tunjung*, Jakarta: Puspa Swara & Rio Tinto Foundation, 1997.

Dyson, Laurentius, and Asharini M. *Tiwah Upacara Kematian pada Masyarakat Dayak Ngaju di Kalimantan Tengah*, Jakarta: P&K, Direktorat Jenderal Kebudayaan, Proyek Media Kebudayaan, 83 p, 1980-81.

Massing, Andreas. "The Journey to Paradise: Funerary Rites of the Benuaq Dayak of East Kalimantan," *Borneo Research Bulletin*, 13 (2): 85-104, 1981.

Massing, Andreas. "Where medicine fails: *belian* disease prevention and curing rituals among the Lawangan Dayak of East Kalimantan," *Borneo Research Bulletin*, 14 (2): 56-84, 1982.

Massing, Andreas. "The journey to paradise: funerary rites of the Benuaq Dayak of East Kalimantan," *Tribus. Jahrbuch des Linden-Museums*, 32: 85-105, 1983.

Sarwoto Kertodipoero. *Kaharingan, Religi dan Penghidupan di Pehuluan Kalimantan*, Bandung: Sumur Bandung, 88 p, 1963.

Schiller, Anne L. *Dynamics of Death: Ritual, Identity, and Religious Change Among the Kalimantan Ngaju*, unpublished PhD thesis, Cornell University, 219 p, 1987.

Weinstock, JA. "Kaharingan: Borneo's 'old religion' becomes Indonesia's newest religion," *Borneo Research Bulletin*, 13 (1): 47-48, 1981.

Weinstock, JA. *Kaharingan and the Luangan Dayaks: Religion and Identity in Central-East Borneo*, unpublished Ph.D. thesis, Cornell University, 244 p, 1983.

Weinstock, JA. "Kaharingan: Life and Death in Southern Borneo," in *Indonesian Religions in Transition*, RS Kipp & S. Rodgers (eds), Tucson: University of Arizona Press, pp 71-97, 1987.

Websites

Articles published in the *Borneo Research Bulletin* can be downloaded from: http://borneoresearchcouncil.org/

Publications from CIFOR (Center for International Forestry Research) can be downloaded from: http://www.cifor.org/

Wikipedia: http://id.wikipedia.org/wiki/Dayak_Benuaq

Biographical Information

Korrie Layun Rampan was born in Samarinda, East Kalimantan, on August 17, 1953, the second son of the adat chief, Paulus Rampan. Both his parents were of Benuaq Dayak ethnicity.

While at university in Yogyakarta, the author joined the literary club Persada Studi Klub, an association that nurtured many of Indonesia's leading poets and writers. Since 1978, he has worked in Jakarta as a book editor, a broadcaster at RRI and TVRI, Indonesia's official radio and televisions stations, respectively, lectured at Semdawar University in West Kutai, East Kalimantan, and held the positions of both Finance Director and Managing Editor of the Jakarta magazine *Sarinah*. As a journalist, he has covered stories on all five continents. Beginning in March 2001, he served as the General Manager/Editor-In-Chief of the Barong Tongkok, West Kutai, Kalimantan newspaper *Sentawar Pos*. In the 2004 general election, he sat for several months as a member of Panwaslu (a watchdog commission for general elections) and then withdrew to run for election to the regional legislature and subsequently sat in the Regional Legislative Council (DPRD) of West Kutai Regency for the period 2004-2009.

However, "Bapak Korrie" has been best known as a literary figure for the 357 books he has written in the areas of science, literature, biography, culture, anthropology, sociology, and children's stories. His novels *Ceremony* and *Fire Cloud Smoke* won prizes at the novel-writing competition of the Jakarta Arts Council in 1976 and 1998, respectively. In 2006, he won the Arts Prize from the Indonesian government in the field of literature. A number of his books have been made essential reading and reference material at elementary, junior and senior high schools, and higher education.

He has also translated about 100 children's stories and numerous short stories by writers from around the world, such as Leo Tolstoy, Knut Hamsen, Anton Chekov, O'Henry, Luigi Pirandello, and others. His works have been selected for dozens of literary anthologies, beginning with *Laut Biru Langit Biru* (*Blue Sea Blue Sky*) edited by Ajit Rosidi (1977),

As of 2013, the author has received sixteen literary and journalistic awards, including the Prize for the Arts from the Indonesian government, the Prize for Culture from the East Kalimantan Provincial Government, and the Prize for Development Journalism from the Republic of Indonesia Ministry of Information. His books have been translated into English, French, and Swedish, among other languages. The French magazine *La Banian* proclaimed him the number one literary critic in Indonesia. For the past several years, he has been writing biographies, history, and on problems of adat, literature, and adat law.

Most recently, he has held the position of Chairman of the Short Story Community of Indonesia, and general manager, editor-in-chief, and the person in charge of the magazine *Suara Borneo*, which is published in Samarinda, East Kalimantan.

George A Fowler lived and traveled widely in the Asia Pacific region for over 30 years, first as a Marine, then as a student of Chinese and Malay, and finally for 23 years as a commercial banker. He co-authored *Pertamina: Indonesian National Oil* and *Java, A Garden Continuum* while living in Indonesia in the early 1970s. George received a Bachelor of Arts from St Michael's College, the University of Toronto, in 1975, and a Master of Arts in International Studies

(China Studies) from the Jackson School of International Studies at the University of Washington in 2002.

He has translated Marah Rusli's classic Indonesian Malay novel *Sitti Nurbaya* (Lontar, 2011), *Old Town* by Chinese writer Lin Zhe (Amazon Crossing, 2011), *The Golden Road* and *Life Under Mao Zedong's Rule* by Hong Kong writer Zhang Da-Peng (CreateSpace, 2012 and 2013, respectively) and *The Rose of Cikembang*, a popular novel of the late 1920's Netherlands East Indies by the Indonesian writer, Kwee Tek Hoay (Lontar, 2013).

George and his wife, Scholastica Auyong, currently live near Seattle, where he is a full-time freelance translator of Chinese, Indonesian, Malay, and Tagalog.

Bernard Sellato, PhD, is the author of *Nomades et sédentarisation à Bornéo*; *Hornbill and Dragon: Arts and Culture of Borneo*; *Nomads of the Borneo Rainforest*; *Borneo: People of the Rainforest*; *Forest, Resources, and People in Bulungan*; and *Innermost Borneo: Studies in Dayak Cultures*. He has written numerous journal articles and is the editor or co-editor of seven books, including *Weights and Measures in Southeast Asia: Metrological Systems and Societies*; *Beyond the Green Myth: Borneo's Hunter-Gatherers in the Twenty-First Century* and, more recently, *Plaited Arts from the Borneo Rainforest* (The Lontar Foundation, 2012). A former director of the Institute of Research on Southeast Asia (CNRS and Université de Provence) in Marseilles, Sellato was the editor of the bilingual journal *Moussons: Social Science Research on Southeast Asia* from 1999 to 2008. Since the early 1970s, he has conducted research in Borneo, first as a geologist and later as a historian and anthropologist.

17 - Need for purification by kinfolk before entering castle
34 - changing ways - presence of white men - dishonor
 to gods + ancestors - missionaries - 36 38
40 - Ompong = potlatch
42 - whites, want to see ceremony - God
48 - healing
 - The theme of ceremonies, as title implies
 runs through - some mystical, some seen as
 boring or artificial by young observer.

104 - Is life a ceremony?

CPSIA information can be obtained at www.ICGtesting.com
Printed in the USA
LVOW10s2053310315

432756LV00001B/63/P

9 789798 083969